CHEYANNA and the HOLEY HORSE

CHEYANNA and the HOLEY HORSE

New York * California

Published by Zippity Books. An imprint of ZLS Publishing

Cover design and illustrations by Kailey Haerr
Edited by: Shannon Johnson, Ashley Minnis-Lemley and Aya Labanieh

Printed in the United States of America

10 9 8 7 6 5 4 3 2 1

ISBN 978-0-9845986-7-0

Library of Congress Control Catalog in Data : 2015948526

For my kids: Lauren, Shana and Shawn who gave me the story, and to all those who share a love of horses.

Chapter 1
The Unexpected Rodeo

I love my old horse, Rocky. He's strong, smart, and the most beautiful horse alive with his black winter coat. The summer's sun turns his hair almost purple, hued like the sunsets.

I'd give anything to ride him today, instead of the buckskin, May-Bee. Rocky is my best friend. He's a friend who never gets tired of doing all the listening, and I never get tired of doing all the talking. He never complains, and thank God for that. Wouldn't that be funny? My horse rolling his eyes at me like my big brother, Jackson, does for talking too much? Imagine if he'd be flaring his nostrils, blowing slobber all over himself, and sticking his chin out at me. Ha! No way. Rocky would never do that!

Rocky's the best friend a teenage girl could have and more. He's my family.

We call him the Rock for a reason. He's never gotten sick, never been crippled. Dad says, "He's the Rock because he's never been hurt a day in his life."

Rocky is still running free in the south pasture, grazing there in order to save on hay, and leaving either May-Bee or my other horse Bucky as my only options to ride today.

I hold my breath as I climb in the saddle, because May-Bee might buck.

Hours into the ride up Rattlesnake Ridge, Jackson and I find two bulls behind the tall brush and turn them down the mountain slope toward our remote ranch home.

"Keep these boys moving, Cheyanna. I'll ride the next ridge and see if there are any others," Jackson says as he swings in the saddle. He points his horse west and hollers, "Be right back. Keep 'em moving, Sis."

I trot May-Bee around the bulls to burn off his extra energy and to keep him from rushing the young animals through the rocks.

For a mountain slope, it's normal to imagine green pine trees and aspen, but not this mountain. Here, we're talking the edge of Wyoming's Rocky Mountains, where sagebrush grows above your horse's head, along with greasewood and buckbrush that'll tear your legs apart at a trot. Boulders are scattered, and the powdered sugar-like sand is so fine that when the wind blows you have no choice but to stand still.

Laced in white, my breath is defined in the cool afternoon air despite the sunshine ablaze overhead. I wish I had worn my heavier coat and—dang, stupid me—a pair of gloves would have been nice. It's springtime weather in the mountains, which is never predictable.

As that thought crosses my mind, May-Bee spooks up the hill for no apparent reason. This horse needs no reason to spook aside from a subtle breeze ruffling

his mane, or a sparrow landing nearby. He dips his head down. His ears lie back as I struggle to pull his head up. With grit in my eyes, I shove my worn boots further into the stirrups and grab hold of May-Bee's black mane. The buckskin twirls around. He points his shoulders down the slope. I reach for the saddlehorn, but grab at empty air. ***Smack***! Air escapes my lungs with a "Humph!" May-Bee's back arches, he lunges once, then again, and another leap knocks the breath from my chest.

I regain my seat in the saddle. Clutching the saddlehorn, I pull May-Bee's head around just as he jerks to the right. In one blink, May-Bee launches me toward the pale sky, so high I feel like I can almost touch the plane passing above me.

Gravity, though, is my foe, and down I smash to the cold, hard earth. Lying motionless, humiliated, and angry upon the rocks, I look up, wishing I could be one of the passengers in that plane overhead, headed anywhere.

My new black Stetson hat rests a step away, the top smashed in with the imprint of a horse's shoe. My breath slows, but my heart continues to race as I think of what would have happened if my head had been in that hat when May-Bee stepped on it.

My wrist throbs. A lone wolf howls from across the ridge. Another, much closer wolf drones her reply. I stand up to scan the hillside. Over my shoulder I see that blasted mule of a horse watching me. "You're done! It's time for a trip to the sale barn," I tell him as I rub my arm. I try to wiggle my fingers and say, "You always were better to look at than to ride."

I edge closer and stand beside the buckskin, take a deep breath, and gnaw my lip. No sign of Jackson yet, and I know I need to find the two young bulls that disappeared when I fell. Dad will be furious with me if I lose them. I lean over and grab one loose rein with my good hand.

"Where's Jackson?" I pull my phone from my denim jacket pocket. My hand begins to tingle as I attempt to text. I move my fingers as much as the pain allows. After I hit send, I gather the second rein and stuff both in my rhinestoned hip pocket. "I can't ride you," I say to May-Bee. I lead him down the slope. Picking and choosing my footing makes the travel slow. May-Bee constantly tries to overcome me and leave. On I walk, wishful but doubtful of seeing my two bulls again.

Dusk creeps on. I turn to May-Bee and toss a rein over each of his shoulders. I have to find those two bovines. Exhaling through clenched teeth, I gather all the courage I have left and grab the saddlehorn. Pulling the reins short, I jab my square-toed boot through the stirrup and climb into the saddle. As I hunt for signs of my two strays, Jackson gallops up the slope.

"Hurry up, Sis," he hollers. "Francis and Sport came to help. We've got your boys at the windmill. I got your message." Jackson rides up beside me. His smile disappears. "Dumped you? You hurt bad?" I nod. Jackson slows to a walk. "Mom'll be home soon. She sent me a text too. She bought two horses. We can finally quit this buckskin beauty. He's better suited for the movies, don't you think?"

We see Mom's headlights blinking between cottonwood trees along the highway. Though the barn and corrals are just a few hundred yards from the house, Dad, Jackson, and I await her arrival near the open barn doors.

We're always on the lookout for the perfect barrel-racing horse, Mom and I, and we're always coming home empty-handed. I hope she finally found the perfect one. I would have been there to choose with her if it hadn't been for school.

I love the rodeo. I'm sure I do. Well, I think I do. Everyone loves the rodeo. The adrenaline, the excitement, the crowds (no, I hate the crowds), and of course, the winning. It hasn't happened for me, the winning. But there is that chance. Mom and Dad were

both rodeo champs; that's how they met. Mom says, "The winning is the best."

I'm really just as happy here at home riding through the hills. I love the open country, the wildflowers, and best of all, that there are no people. I hate all those people watching me ride. That's the worst. I prefer it to be just my horse, Rocky, and me.

We stand in the light of the old log barn, waiting. I jump up and down because I'm cold, not because I'm excited to see the new horses. In fact, the idea of a new horse depresses me because it means it's time to give up my old Rocky.

I bet Jackson can't wait to tell Mom about my impromptu rodeo in the rocks on crazy May-Bee. Any horse will be an improvement over him after today's fiasco.

"We want to keep them separate down here for a couple of weeks. They might have picked up an illness from the sale barn," Dad explains to us, as if we don't know.

"We know, Dad," Jackson says and reminds Dad that we're both teenagers now and have seen many horses bought through the sale barn.

I stand shivering as Jackson comes close and bumps my shoulder. He slugs me softly and says, "Come on, Sis. Put up your dukes! Box with me, it'll keep you warm." He bounces around, not waiting for my reply, and says, "Dad checked you out, your wrist's not broken. Cheer up and box me."

Finally, the truck is creeping up the lane. "Knock it off, Jackson." I roll my eyes. "Oh man! Hurry up and get here!"

Chapter 2
The New Horses

The old Ford, rickety and loud, finally pulls up to the barn. I see my baby sister, Cora, who looks like my identical twin aside from the eight years between us. Her smiling, round face is pressed against the truck's window.

Dad beats us all to the trailer door. The palomino horse is the first to unload. Mom climbs out of the cab, holding Cora in her arms. She ambles back to the open trailer.

"We sure did miss you all. To Montana and back is too long a trip for just Cora and me. We are beat!" Mom exhales slowly. "Whoever thought to have horse sales in the middle of calving season obviously doesn't own livestock," she says. "We'll never make that trip alone again."

"I knew I should have gone with you two, Mom," I say. "Staying here alone with this dude," pointing to Jackson, "was all I can handle; I hope I'll never have do that again, either!"

Dad takes Cora in his arms. "Are you happy to be home, little lady? I missed you so much." He snuggles her. Dad holds Cora over his head. Her soft curls spill from beneath her hat and fall across his face. He pulls her down, covering her with whiskery kisses. Muffled in squeals of laughter, Cora attempts her protest.

"He looks stout," Dad says, as he pats the palomino with Cora on his hip. "Has he been around livestock, did they say?" he asks, giving the lead rope to Jackson.

"Yeah, the palomino has seen cows some. They claim that he's an all-around cow pony," Mom says, turning toward Jackson. "You ought to make a rodeo horse out of him. He's young and needs a good rider to handle him. Yeller is his name," she says as Francis, our hired man, walks from the barn. Sport, his mangy little terrier with a missing ear, scampers close behind.

Francis has been here longer than any of us, working on the ranch. My grandpa found him abandoned and wandering through town. When my grandpa tried to find out more about him, he learned that the kid didn't think like everybody else. He had a mental disability. Gramps knew that Francis was smart and special in his own way and hired the kid. Dad says he doesn't remember the place without Francis. He's like my dad's brother in a way.

"Sure, I'll give him a go. Looks like a good one. Way to go, Mom!" Jackson takes the young horse and leads him in circles. "I'll try any horse, Mom, other than that crazy May-Bee. He tried to kill Cheyanna today. We're done with him. Cheyanna got back on him, though." Jackson smiles. "You should've seen her, Mom. She's like a professional bronc-rider. Isn't she, Francis?"

"All right, that's enough," I say, glancing through the openings along the trailer walls. "Neither of you saw me get bucked off today; it wasn't that dramatic." I catch two big eyes watching me through the trailer's slats. The horse bats long, dark eyelashes, and the large white stripe down his red face stands out in the darkness. I'm tired of hearing about Jackson's rendition of my "near-death experience," as he's been calling it. "Let's see this second new horse," I say and hop into the open trailer where I see Mom has gift-wrapped him for me with a big bow around his neck. I smile at the effort she put into making him look special.

"I'm just glad you got back on the bugger, Chey. You braver'n me," Francis says, scooping Sport into his arms.

The smell of urine and fresh manure compels me to quickly untie the rope from the trailer wall and get back out to the open air. Before I turn to leave, the big red horse nudges me with his nose. Losing my balance for a moment, I slip backward, bumping into his large frame. The horse is solid behind me and doesn't spook from my sudden movements. Instead, he lowers his head and nuzzles against me, and the bow rustles quietly.

From outside of the trailer, Francis peers through the opening. He hangs there awhile, studying the horse with me, before saying, "Chey, he a good horse for you." The huge horse steps to nuzzle Francis through the trailer's slats. "Yes, sir. I mean ma'am." Francis chuckles and buries his face in the crook of his arm. He lifts his head up, leaving his smile behind, and says, "This horse can be your friend, Chey." The chestnut horse and Francis continue their own conversation, seemingly understanding exactly what the other is saying.

I overhear Mom outside say, "Yeller's got heavy, strong legs. Put him in the pasture for a while and we'll see what he amounts to." I peer outside the trailer to see Mom talking with her hands. Looking at Dad and Jackson, she says, "You two boys take Cora inside. She's hungry and tired. Francis and I will stay and help Cheyanna turn the new horses out—"

"No," Dad interrupts. "We want to get a look at Cheyanna's horse too. You go on down with Cora. I know that you're both tired. Do you not want us seeing him or something, Bea?" Dad asks, and winks at Mom.

"No...well." She hesitates. "He's unique, Joe," she answers. "I want to let Cheyanna get a chance to look him over, that's all. He's got a..."

Mom mumbles something as I lead the horse to stand in the beam of the truck's lights, his hooves clip-clapping against the gravel road.

"He's a good-looking horse," I say. "Mom, I think our quest to find a new horse is over! He's got the perfect build with those long legs. I like him, but... still, I don't want to give up old Rocky." I can feel a nervous lump in the back of my throat, and I swallow a gulp of air. Wiping my face with the back of my leather glove, I struggle for some control. "How old did you say he is, anyway?" I ask as I reach up on tiptoes to stroke the big animal's shoulder and comb my fingers through his silky mane.

Before Mom answers, Jackson says, "Look at his size! I can make a roping horse out of him. Trade you, Cheyanna." Jackson leads his palomino into the light to compare the horse's sizes. "He's too big a horse for a tiny pint like you. "

"No way, Bro!" I squeeze the cotton rope firmly in my cold fist. "He's a beautiful horse, Mom. I do like him," I add, trying not to sound ungrateful. I walk him toward the barn and away from Jackson's sticky fingers.

"He's seven," Mom says. "His name is BigHorn. BigHornCatchMeQuick." Following us to the barn, she says, "He is a little thin from competing. He was winning high school rodeos all over Montana before his owner got a new horse for college. We'll get some weight back on him before your season starts."

Dad hurries little Cora's short legs to the barn. When they reach the barn, he says, "If he doesn't work out for you, Cheyanna, I don't think you'll have to beg Jackson to take him off your hands." Dad turns to Mom, and says, "Bea, he's a good-looking horse. He might be more like an arena horse than the young palomino. I know Cheyanna is eager to get him going on the barrels, but she isn't ready for old Rocky to retire." Dad looks toward me, and says, "I've got a suggestion. I know you love him, but I want you to find Rocky a new home. Now, before you say anything, hear me out. You know the Erickson girls down river will keep him racing in the Little Britches Rodeos this summer. That way he isn't completely retiring, but he's not competing with our younger horses."

I stand motionless, holding the new horse's lead rope. The world comes to a pause. "Dad, I can't sell Rocky so suddenly, not yet, not ever! Can't Rocky just retire here on the ranch? He deserves that," I plead. "Can't we just sell crazy May-Bee instead?"

I can't let Rocky go. I've never ridden any other horse in a rodeo. I've never ridden any other horse in front of a crowd. Ride in front of a crowd on a new horse? No way.

Dad keeps his eyes in Mom's direction when he says, "You know good and well that May-Bee doesn't compete and is for cattle round up. Not to mention, you'll always choose to ride Rocky over the new horse. The new horse is going to need a lot more of your time and energy to train well for competitions."

Dad scratches his balding head. "By the way, why *are* you so worried about BigHorn, Beatrice?" he asks

quickly, changing the subject. "What makes him so unique?"

Dad doesn't notice the tears welling up in my eyes. I shake my head in disbelief. Francis steps closer to me and pats my new horse's shoulder.

"Dad already wants me to sell Rocky," I whisper to Francis. I knew this was going to happen, but I never imagined it would come about so fast. Mom takes three steps closer to me. I presume she's coming to my rescue, but she doesn't.

She stops, unties the bow around BigHorn's neck and says, "BigHorn is unique... He is unique because he breathes through a tracheotomy, a permanent hole cut in his windpipe under his chin."

Chapter 3
The Horse With the Hole In His Neck

I feel the warmth of BigHorn's massive body radiating beside me. The empty night leaves room for the quiet breathing of a now less-than-perfect horse. My raging heart beats in a confusing rhythm. Attempting to smile in Mom's direction, I lick my lips and taste the salt of tears.

Before any of us can question what Mom said, she explains, "His nasal passages collapsed two years ago and a permanent tracheotomy, done by a vet in Denver, helps him to breathe." She looks down and scuffs her boots in the loose dirt. I hear her sigh before she says, "It was that or put him to sleep. He is too good a horse to put down."

As Mom smiles towards me, her shoulders drop a little. "Cheyanna, any other horse with his training and winning record would cost a small fortune. The girl who sold him was running him in the high school rodeo circuit. His racing experience is priceless." Mom looks toward Dad. "Joe, this horse is a winning athlete."

The new horse nudges me with his nose, knocking me backwards a step. I feel no warmth coming from his chestnut muzzle. He steps closer and nudges me a second time, as if saying, "Come on, won't you play with me?" He reminds me of a lonely little kid nobody picks for their team. I step close, and he presses his warm head to my belly. "Hi, you." I rub the white blaze down his face. "You're okay here," I whisper. Francis smiles his honest smile and continues patting the horse's shoulder. I study Francis whiskered face, looking for some sign of disgust or disapproval, but I know that Francis deeply loves all living creatures. He would never be disgusted by something like a tracheotomy.

"No matter what you say, Bea, he is disabled, not a winner." I hear Dad grumble. "This horse is defective. Come on, girls. Let's go to the house." Dad hefts Cora higher into his arms and takes a step towards me. "No one wants to ride a horse with a gaping hole in its throat. I'll take him up the canyon tomorrow and put him out of his misery." He grabs the lead rope from my hand and shoves it toward Francis. "Put him in the corral, would you please, Francis?" Dad steers me toward the open barn door. I walk with Dad and Cora from the barn. My thoughts grind like the earth beneath my boots, fueling my frustration. Distracted as I am by BigHorn's condition, it takes a minute for Dad's threat to sink in.

I wriggle free from Dad's grasp. He looks at me with a furrowed brow. I hesitate one moment before I say, "Dad, you can't shoot my new horse." I spin away. Without waiting for his protest, I run back to the barn.

This hole thing is fine; I mean, who really cares? I roll my eyes. Why is everyone making such a big deal of it? Does this hole affect his running ability? No, Mom says he's been competing for two years. Heading to the barn, toward Jackson's and Mom's voices, I glance up toward the twinkling night. "I don't want to sell Rocky, I love him, but Dad's fix is just to shoot the poor new horse! Well, that's not going to happen," I tell myself.

Mom and Jackson are putting things away in the barn; the door of the tack room creaks, and their voices echo inside. "Give him a chance, Jackson. BigHorn is a fine horse," I hear her say.

"I don't know, Mom. He's got a hole in his throat!" Jackson says. "The flies will bug him. Flies bug. Get it? Flies are bugs!" Jackson laughs at his own attempt at a joke, then asks Mom, "What if he chokes on a fly? Then they'll really bug him."

I hear the rattling of a bucket handle and the clink-clank of a tin coffee can being tossed back into the grain bin.

"Stop that now, mister!" Mom sounds mad. "You are not funny, and this is not a joke! We've been hunting for months for a younger horse for Cheyanna. A horse that she can win on!"

Hearing my name as I hike to the barn, I hurry toward the open door. Neither Mom nor Jackson notice me, so I clear my throat with a deliberate, yet ineffective, cough.

"Yeah, any race with him would be neck and neck thanks to the hole in his neck." Jackson laughs.

"Excuse me, Jackson. I can hear you!" I shout. I glance at Mom, who raises her arm and wipes her forehead. Rubbing her chin with the back of her hand,

she pinches her lips together and says, "This horse is Cheyanna's chance, Jackson, to finally win." Mom grins toward me, takes a deep breath and says, "Please don't make accepting this new horse any harder on her than it already is; it's tough enough with Rocky getting too old to rodeo."

"Okay, Mom. I won't. I promise." Jackson gives me a wink. "Dad doesn't like the horse, though," he says. "And ***he*** isn't going to make accepting him easy. Honestly, though, I can't imagine that he'd shoot him, Chey." Jackson smiles at me and shrugs. "He'd rather you keep riding old Rocky than ride a faulty horse in a rodeo, because you know how important appearances are to him. Maybe I can still ride him, though. People watching my four seconds of roping is different than watching your twenty seconds of barrel racing."

Mom shakes her head. "The hole, the trachea, doesn't make him faulty; it just makes him different." She ignores the dilemma about Dad and says, "BigHorn is a horse with a natural ability and willingness to run. All he needs now is a brave girl. He needs someone with enough guts and love to take him and let him run." Looking to Jackson, she adds, "This horse has lived with the tracheotomy for two years and will continue to live with it. You don't need to do anything for him, aside from an occasional cleaning."

Jackson's reminder of the crowds at the rodeo makes me suddenly realize I don't want to be seen on a horse like BigHorn. "Well, he isn't my horse, Jackson. You can have the holey horse! I don't want him. I'm keeping old Rocky!" I shout as I leave the barn. I dash from the barn and find Francis standing in the corral talking to the new horses, Sport by his side as always. I try to hear what Francis is saying, but I can't make out his words. Instead, I only hear the voices from the barn. I'm not certain what is said, but I can hear Jackson snicker.

I hear Mom say, "Your teasing didn't help things, Jackson. She was probably coming up here to look him over more. I'm going to go to the house. Please turn off the lights when you're done with your chores."

Francis mumbles again to the big red horse. I still can't make out what he's saying. He walks to the fence and climbs over. Francis rests his big hand on my head, like he's done since I was small before telling me something insightful. He smiles and nods, but only says, "Good night, yes it is. I'dda better get on home." With that, he walks behind the barn to the bunkhouse.

Mom steps from the barn and hollers, "Hey, Cheyanna! Oh, I didn't know you were so close." She smiles and says, "Come along, let's walk together to the house."

I know the conversation that awaits me as I walk, so I make a point of trailing behind Mom while scrolling through my cell phone. I don't need to hear any more tonight. I heard enough in the barn, listening to Mom and Jackson. Let Jackson have the horse. I am happy riding good old Rocky forever—he'll never be the center of all the jokes. Rocky is the best dang horse on the ranch, and the whole family knows it. Dad can't just decide to sell him without my say. I never imagined I'd have to sell him so soon.

I only look up from my phone when I bump into Mom. "Oh! Why'd you stop?"

She puts her hand across my phone's screen and says, "I wish you had been with me and Cora at the auction today. We missed you." We begin walking, more slowly, toward the house.

"Yeah, I wish I had been there too. I would have picked out a better horse," I retort.

Mom frowns before sighing, "He's a good horse, Cheyanna."

I shove my phone in my coat pocket. We walk silently in the dark for a few minutes. "Hey, Mom."

"Yeah?"

"Don't let Dad shoot the horse."

Mom swings her arm across me as we climb the steps. "He won't, kiddo. He's just upset about the money." She squeezes my shoulder and adds, "Don't you worry, Chey. You're going to win on this horse."

Chapter 4
A Home for BigHorn

Dad sits at the kitchen table stirring his steaming cup of cocoa, and Cora eats the marshmallows from hers as Mom and I come into the house.

A fire crackles and pops from the wood stove. "Are you drinking the hot chocolate too, or just eating the little marshmallows?" I ask Cora as I hurry through the kitchen in an attempt to avoid Dad.

I walk into my bedroom and shut the door behind me. I don't want a new horse. Why should I have to sell my Rocky? The question rings through my mind as I pace the wooden floor. "Stupid me, snap out of it, Cheyanna! You can figure out a plan," I tell myself as I rush to my wallet that is stashed in the bookshelf. I pull out my cash. I'll buy Rocky from Dad before he sells him. "Then he won't be so upset about the money and BigHorn either," I say out loud.

I sit to count the money and hear a light *tap-tap-tap* on my door. I turn and ask, "Who is it?"

The door opens slightly, and two big brown eyes peek through the crack. "Cheynni, can I come in and see you?" Cora whispers. "You want some cocoa?"

I shove the loose bills in my pocket, then rush to scoop up my baby sis. "Of course I do, squirt." I hug her close before setting her down on her feet. Cora's tiny, warm hand leads me back to the kitchen.

"Your cup is in the microwave, Cheyanna," Dad tells me. "I put some coffee on too, Bea."

Two cups of hot chocolate later, Mom and I sit in the bathroom while Cora bathes. I sit on the floor and reach over the tub. At my touch, a tiny toy whale leaps and dives in the soapy water, splashing us all. We turn as Dad comes in and leans against the porcelain sink.

"I'm worried about this horse, girls. You're not going to ride a horse in public with such an appearance, are you, Chey?" Dad doesn't wait for my response and says, "I know how kids are sometimes, when someone or something is ugly. I wouldn't ride a horse like that." He stares down to the cold linoleum. "Cheyanna, you don't want to ride an ugly horse, do you?"

Mom opens her mouth to speak, but Dad raises his hand, turns toward me, and says, "You're not going to ride him. Find him a home tomorrow, or I will." He leaves the bathroom without looking either of us in the eye and closes the door.

I holler, "Does this mean you're not going to shoot him?"

"Wait a minute, Joe," Mom shouts. "You're not being fair to Cheyanna. She deserves the opportunity to try BigHorn." Mom jumps to her feet, dropping a folded towel to the floor. Bending to pick it up, she adds, "She deserves to win."

Dad yells from the kitchen, "Cheyanna deserves a horse that she's not embarrassed to ride!"

We hear him slamming cupboards as he says, "No daughter of mine will ride a defective horse like him in a rodeo!"

The furrow between my eyes fuels a headache. I try to relax and toss my head back to stare at the condensation collecting on the ceiling. I'm not embarrassed by BigHorn, but should I be?

We finish giving Cora her bath while she tells me about her trip. Once we dress her in her pajamas, Cora asks me to read her a story.

"Sure I will," I smile. "Now, get in your bed. I'll only read you one." I wait for her usual protest, because she loves books as much as I do, but tonight her only response is a great big yawn. I only read half of the story before she falls asleep. I turn off the light and tiptoe to my own book.

Hours after laying my book down, the house is empty of voices. I just can't stop thinking about BigHorn. Will Dad really kill BigHorn? Is the hole that big? Will people really notice it?

I slide out of my warm bed, and head to the porch. My boots feel cold and damp without socks. Grabbing a flashlight, I plunge into my parka and gently unlatch the door with a crack just big enough for me to maneuver outside and up to the corrals.

I stand next to the fence, resting my head on the wooden pole. I spot BigHorn and say, "I see you there, you big chestnut horse." He raises his head toward my voice.

I climb up the corral rails. Hoisting my leg over, I sit on the top pole shining my flashlight down, blanketing BigHorn in its glow. He prances around in the light. His long tail looks like flowing honey trailing behind him. "From here, BigHorn, you look like the perfect horse," I say. "You sure are the quiet type. Oh my, I bet you can't talk, can you?" I gasp. I remember Mom telling me that he can't nicker because his nasal passages are collapsed. He tries to show me he is happy to see me by swishing his tail and pawing the ground.

I slide quietly from the fence, eager to get closer. He stands facing me without a hint that he might retreat. I hum softly as I approach him with my open hand. He's not spooked by my presence. I imagine that he's showing off, trying to get me to like him, perhaps. He stands still. "I should have brought you a treat, boy. I wish I had thought of that earlier." I stand at his side and raise my mittened hand to stroke his shoulder.

"Someone, somewhere, must have really loved you to keep you running." I inch closer. "They either loved you, or you are super fast!"

I shine my light beneath his jawbone, directly where his throat begins. The hole is larger than I'd imagined. I touch the opening gently. The surrounding hair is wet, warm, and matted slightly. I look deep into his windpipe and the red flesh glistens in the spotlight. BigHorn's breath is unlabored and steady, and the suture line surrounding the healed edge is scarred yet smooth.

I pull my mittens off, and stuff them into the pockets of my coat. What will people think about me riding a horse with such a huge gouge in its throat? What will people say? I push the ugly thoughts from my mind. Lifting my hand, I reach to feel him again. He steps closer.

"You're as soft as a kitten." BigHorn pushes his nose against my chest as if asking to be ridden. "No, boy, I have to get to bed. At least now that I've seen you more closely, I can sleep. You're a nice horse, and I don't want you to die."

I stand there stroking the horse's silky coat. I force my exhausted eyelids to stay open as I find my way back to the house.

I wake to the smell of breakfast. Sitting up quickly, I look down at my watch. Loose curls spill into my eyes. The bright morning sunshine fills the room. I stretch as I climb from the covers. The roar of Dad's truck reminds me what I dread about this day. I don't have much time. I quickly dress, rush through the kitchen, grab a slice of bacon, and run outside to see Dad's dust billowing behind the horse trailer.

"He didn't give me a chance to find BigHorn a home," I grumble. The bacon churns in my empty stomach as my mind goes wild with possibilities of Dad's destination. The realization that he must have found BigHorn a home settles my anger... slightly. He wouldn't need the trailer if he had put BigHorn "out of his misery."

I plod up the path to the corrals, dragging my feet in the loose gravel. The sun, climbing higher into the morning sky, burns hot on my face.

The barn echoes with my footsteps and my voice hollering, "Mom, Jackson, Francis, where are you? Is anybody here?"

Fearful of what I will find—or whom I won't—move swiftly through the empty barn and out to the corral. BigHorn stands nibbling on the hay scattered in the feed bunk. The young palomino, Yeller, stands beside him.

"Thank God!" My heart quiets. "You're here. What a relief!" I rush to BigHorn and lay my arm across his back. I don't have much time to find him a home. I gently stroke his mane, then hurry back toward the house.

Bursting back in the kitchen to find more breakfast, I find Jackson sitting at the table spooning heaps of sugar into a coffee cup.

"Hey, about time you got here. Where've you been?" He gulps the sugary coffee.

"Where did Dad go with the trailer?" I plop down on a chair across from Jackson, ignoring his question. "I bet that's your third spoon of sugar, huh?" Watching him drink the syrupy mixture makes my teeth ache.

"Dad and Francis went to Aunt Katie's to get a cow. He said to find that horse a home before they get back." Jackson pushes the cup toward me, but keeps the spoon and dips it into the sugar bowl again. Smiling, he pops it into his mouth.

"I can't do that! Aunt Katie lives only an hour away. They've already been gone ten minutes." Wringing my hands, I rise and walk to look out the kitchen window. "Did Francis say anything about the horse?"

"No, what would Francis know about horses with holes? Holey horses... He's no priest! What would he know about holy horses?" Jackson laughs.

"Francis doesn't know things like you and I do, Jackson. You know that he's wired a little differently, but he truly understands all animals. He wanted to say something last night about BigHorn, but he didn't." Taking a deep breath, I turn away from the window. "Help me out here, Jackson, who will take BigHorn? Who will take good care of him?" I pace the tiled floor.

"Call your friend Jasmine. She's a barrel racer," Jackson says, clenching the spoon in his teeth.

"No! I am not giving her a horse with a giant hole in his throat!" I sit across from Jackson.

"Why, Cheyanna? What does his hole have to do with how good a horse he is?" He takes the spoon from his mouth and licks his lips. "That hole is permanent. It's how he breathes. It's part of him," Jackson says matter-of-factly.

"Because, it's ugly and embarrassing, and I'm not asking my friend to take care of him. I don't imagine

Jazz would like him anyway. I'm not so sure she would treat him well. Remember, she always chooses her horses based on their appearance."

Jackson shakes his head. "I was just watching him this morning when I fed them some hay. He's a good-looking horse. Jasmine will want him, I bet. Then you won't have to sell Rocky."

"No, I'm definitely not giving BigHorn to Jazz. I know what she's like. We need another plan."

Jackson pushes away from the table. "Well, we could just hide him in one of the back pastures. You could ride him out. I'll come get you in a couple of hours," he says as he walks to the sink and tosses his spoon in with a clank.

"I wish! But Dad will see him. It's just a matter of time. Besides, BigHorn would eventually get in a band of wild horses out in the foothills. The wild studs would kill him."

"Who else barrel races or rodeos? Who wants to rodeo and needs a horse?" Jackson asks. Then he snaps his fingers theatrically. "I don't know, but I do know someone who will know: Coach Phillip. Coach is always taking in old horses for the rodeo team." He flips open his cell phone and grins.

I march outside to wait. The fresh air feels cooler than the kitchen, and for the first time this morning, my stomach stops gurgling.

Jackson rushes out behind me. "He isn't home. Now what?"

"Let's take BigHorn to his place anyway. We'll have time to explain everything when we get there," I say, smiling, relieved to have a plan. "I bet Coach is just

outside, feeding his own horses."

"We'd better get going, it's a long ride. We don't have the truck and trailer because Dad took it to Aunt Katie's. Here's your chance to ride him at least," Jackson says with a big grin.

"No! You ride him." I don't want anyone to see me. I'd be too embarrassed.

Chapter 5
Trouble at Coach's Place

Jackson and I leave the ranch for Coach Phillip's place as the sun nears its highest peak. The horses amble along, twitching their tails. We ride along without speaking, listening to the clinking tune of a loose horseshoe. Jackson swings his lariat over his head and throws it around every brush we pass. He and BigHorn begin a game of sagebrush roping. I roll my eyes, hoping it doesn't last for the entire seven-mile ride.

I am glad Jackson is riding BigHorn. I love old Rocky, with his smooth stride and easy-going attitude. I smile, my determination to keep him stronger than ever.

"Jackson, if we don't find a home for him you should rope on BigHorn this season," I say, the idea suddenly occurring to me. "You'll want to keep him at Coach Phillip's place, though. Coach will help you get him tuned up, and Dad won't have to look at him."

Jackson turns in the saddle and says, "Let's see how quick he'll stop for me, Sis." Jackson spurs BigHorn forward, standing in his stirrups and leaning over the horse's shoulders as the big horse lunges into a gallop. Dust and pebbles spray behind him as BigHorn sprints down the road.

"Thanks for the warning. I'm eating gravel here." Rocky pulls against his bit, wanting to race. I pull firmly on the reins and persuade him to stay behind.

Hundreds of feet ahead, Jackson sits back into the saddle. I hear him say, "Whoa, boy." In a single heartbeat, BigHorn is motionless.

I ride up beside them. The smile on Jackson's face mirrors my own. I continue toward Coach's corrals, thrilled with the notion that Jackson, not I, will prove BigHorn's abilities to Dad in front of all those people.

Jackson says, "Dad said he doesn't want his daughter riding a defective horse in a rodeo. He never said anything about his son."

"And you're not embarrassed to ride him?"

Jackson, looking me dead in the eyes, says, "No, Cheyanna. I'm not a bit ashamed to ride BigHorn. Because we're going to win."

We trot on toward Coach's place. The sun peaks above our heads. "I wish we'd brought some water along," I say, licking my parched lips.

We urge our steeds into a canter. The scenery isn't as noticeable, but the faster motion feels invigorating as the horses kick up sand.

We round the final bend to Coach's Thunderbird Ranch and slow our horses to a rapid walk, hoping not to startle Coach's pack of dogs. Jackson glances around. "Coach Phillip will be excited to see me riding a horse like BigHorn. You know, with the horse's strange hole being so scientific and all."

Coach Phillip is Mr. Phillip during biology class. He is my teacher this year, my first year of junior high school, but Jackson had him last year in seventh grade, too.

The usual welcoming committee of hounds and mutts is nowhere to be seen. I look to Jackson for his reaction. "The horses are all corralled down by the barn," I say, pointing ahead to the shut gate.

"Where are all the dogs?" Jackson asks.

"Coach must have them with him. Come on, Jackson."

The unusual quiet resonates. Feeling like an intruder, my senses are heightened.

"Yeah, you're probably right. We should have brought paper and a pen to leave a note in case he isn't here," Jackson says.

"But what would you write? 'Here's an ugly horse for you to keep for us to practice on, Coach. Our dad won't have him on our ranch!' Something like that, huh?"

"Oh, Cheyanna, you make it sound so bad."

"It is that bad, Jackson."

"Chey, it's no big deal. We ride our horses over to the Thunderbird Arena to practice every season. This year we'll just be keeping our horses here like most everyone else." Jackson stops BigHorn in the road before adding, "Everyone else on the rodeo team uses Coach's stables. Why shouldn't we?"

We ride along through the silence. Finally, the quiet is broken by a horse's heavy stomp in the distance. A dog whimpers from the opposite end of the barn, near the round-pen.

No words are spoken as our eyes meet. I feel a hurricane of butterflies in my stomach. We race to the barn in a cloud of dust, leap from our saddles and run around to the back of the red barn. I realize I've been holding my breath. I take a deep gulp of air as we see Coach's old scruffy dog, Marge, coming to greet us. The other two woolly dogs lie whimpering outside the circular pen of aged pine poles.

We discover Coach Phillip face-down in the center of the pen. A black colt paws the dirt two strides away, kicking dust into the air. His saddle clings to the side of his wet belly and his bridle, torn free from his ears, dangles from his sweaty neck. I hear soft moans coming from the center of the pen. "Jackson, run to the house. Call an ambulance!" I yell as I open the wooden gate.

Standing frozen, Jackson doesn't move.

"Go, Jackson! Run to the house. Call 911! He's hurt bad and has probably been like this all morning, maybe since yesterday. Hurry!" I shout.

Jackson leaps to a sprint; a young shaggy dog runs behind, barking. I hear the wooden screen door slam.

I open the heavy gate and the young horse charges away from Coach. I hear Coach moan and rush to kneel beside him in the dust. Resting my open palm on his back, I say, "Hey, Coach. It's me, Cheyanna. Can you hear me?" I brush the loose dirt away from his nose. Brown stains streak Coach's face and a red pool collects beneath his mouth. "Think, Cheyanna, think. You know what to do. I remember ABC. Airway, breathing and..." I watch my hand subtly rise and then fall as his lungs labor to fill and empty of air.

"Help is on the way!" I hear Jackson yell.

I look up as Jackson jogs the hundred yards from the house.

"Don't try to move him!" he hollers as he races to the pen. "Wipe the dirt away from his face." Jackson slips through the fence railings.

Coach suddenly coughs. "Jackson, that you? What day is it?" Coach's voice is just a whisper.

Jackson kneels beside us. "Today is Sunday, Coach. How long have you been out here?" Coach doesn't reply. "Keep talking to him, Cheyanna," Jackson says. "That's important, it'll keep him conscious." Jackson wipes his own face with the back of his hand. I see sweat glistening across his forehead.

"Sure good to see you kids," Coach says, then he falls silent again. He squeezes my hand as he shuts his

eyes. We sit beside him, watching and waiting. Coach licks his lips and breathes, his face pinched in agony. He whispers, "You two, please feed..." He groans. "My dogs."

We assure him we will do so just before he passes out.

Jackson looks at me wide-eyed and grimacing and says, "Cheyanna, why didn't we bring a phone? Keep talking to him; I'll run back to the house and pass on updates to the emergency operator." Hopping to his feet, Jackson races back to the telephone.

Sitting in the dirt, not sure what to do, I tell Coach, "We got this new horse named BigHorn. He has a bizarre condition. He is beautiful, though. He's a big horse; he has long legs and one white sock." Looking up toward the house, I pray, "Hurry, Jackson." Turning my attention back to Coach, I say, "Dad said he will sell Rocky. But that was before Dad knew BigHorn was defective. Things seem to be working out fine because now Jackson plans on roping on BigHorn if you'll let him hide him here." I sigh. "I want to ride BigHorn, too. I know I'd win on him, but I'm embarrassed to ride him. What would people say? Not to mention, if I accept BigHorn as my new horse, I'll have to say good-bye to Rocky."

Pursing my lips, I gaze to the tops of the distant cottonwood trees. "Coach, I wish I could ride both horses, forever, but only on the ranch." I pause before confessing, "I don't enjoy riding in the rodeo. I am always afraid of what the crowds will think. I race for Dad... Mom too, I guess." The silence falls heavily around me.

Suddenly, a hacking sound begins to come from Coach's mouth. The coughing starts with a wheeze and grows deeper, consuming Coach's entire body. Jackson is racing from the house when I look up. The coughing stops as Jackson reaches the fence. "I feel so helpless, Jackson. What more can we do?" I ask.

Jackson announces, running back into the corral, "The helicopter has been dispatched from Billings. It's due to arrive here any minute."

"Coach," I say, leaning closer, "we'll feed the horses and dogs every day and we'll start riding here too." I squeeze his cold hand and whisper, "I promise."

"We're to keep his mouth and nose clear of dirt, not to try moving him, and keep him as warm as possible." Jackson licks his lips and scratches his head. "How should we keep him warm? Does he feel cold to you?"

Reaching over his still body, I feel the side of his chilled face. "Yes, he's very cold. Blankets, we need blankets." I jump up, remembering how Mom warms us with blankets fresh from the dryer. "Jackson, go find some quilts and throw them in the dryer."

We run back and forth countless times bringing warm blankets to drape over our chilled patient. Jackson and I tell Coach more about our holey horse as the faint drum of the distant rescue helicopter fills the sky.

Chapter 6
Hiding BigHorn

Francis doesn't drive on the highways. He doesn't have a driver's license, but he comes to Coach's place and picks me and Jackson up when we call him anyway.

Francis arrives at the Thunderbird Ranch moments after the helicopter leaves for town. He helps Jackson take care of Coach's colt, who is crazy with fright, and helps me find stalls for BigHorn and Rocky.

"Chey, that good that you bring BigHorn here to Coach's. To ride him in the arena."

"Yeah, Francis," Jackson interrupts, "we're going to keep Bighorn here during rodeo season." Jackson grins. Our secret to ride BigHorn is safe with Francis, although we never mention it is a secret.

We arrive home with just enough light in the western sky to see us through our evening chores. Dad is corralling a couple of heavy, soon-to-be calving first-time heifers. These young moms-to-be will need some extra help giving birth, and maybe even more help adjusting to motherhood.

Jackson and I finish feeding Yeller and May-Bee some fresh hay with Dad's help. May-Bee prances in circles around Yeller, showing off his beautiful mane. Yeller, though, has taken to Dad and steps inches behind him, nuzzling his back and nearly stepping on his heels.

"When do you think Coach will be back, Dad?" Jackson asks.

"He'll be home soon. He's got a colt waiting at home for him to ride," replies Dad. "I never meant for you kids to take BigHorn to the Thunderbird Ranch, but I sure am glad that you did." Dad turns and pushes the yellow horse away.

"You kids better start riding these fat horses too before rodeo season gets rolling," Dad tells us. "You got a letter in the mail today from the Junior Rodeo Association. I bet it's your spring rodeo schedule." He reaches down, midstride, to pick up a hay-bale string

and says, "I'll haul Yeller and some hay to Coach's place. If you're there doing chores every afternoon, you may as well be riding there, too."

Jackson and I exchange knowing glances, but neither of us lets our ideas be known to Dad. Smiling, Jackson says, "Sure, Dad, that might work out fine. I know my buddies plan to bring horses to Coach's arena, too. Steve has some steers that he wants to get moved over there for roping practice this week."

Dad softly brushes my hand with his worn leather glove.

"Cheyanna, is there anyone you know on the team that will be riding at Phillip's arena?" Dad asks.

"Yeah, Jasmine will be riding there. She hasn't brought her horse over yet, though."

"That's what I thought. Well, I'd better give your coach a heads-up. We can't have all you kids riding there alone every day. I'll go visit Coach Phillip at the hospital before I bring over the other horse; I'm thinking on a solution," he says. Fumbling with the chain on the gate, Dad adds, "Hiding BigHorn at the Thunderbird Ranch does not count as finding him a new home, kids." Dad shoves the steel gate open and strides away.

Chapter 7
The Hospital Visit

Jackson and I check up on Coach's place each day after school as March turns to April. We plan daily roping and barrel racing practice there for the spring season. It is still too early to put these plans together, and with heavy rain each afternoon, the weather is not conducive to an outdoor arena.

The aroma of dinner fills the air as we come into the house. The strong smells are nauseating; I can't eat a single bite. Looking up from my plate, my eyes meet Mom's.

"Are you feeling sick?" she asks. "You look a bit pale."

"Yes, I feel a little sick. May I be excused?" I ask as I rise from the table and take my plate to the kitchen sink. "I'm going outside for a minute for some fresh air." I slip outside to get away from the agonizing smell of food. Here in the open, I feel more in control of my thoughts. I start walking around the house and somehow I end up at the woodpile. Heaping my arms full of chopped wood to carry in for the fire, I haul load after load to the porch. I feel revived by the physical exertion. A flicker of movement catches my eye, and I look up to see Jackson standing on the porch. He holds his hands over his belly and chuckles.

"Feeling better?" Jackson asks. "We have plenty of wood in the house for a few days. Why are you hauling it? Mom can't ever get you to bring in wood, yet here you are hauling in piles without being asked."

"Oh, Jackson, I'm just worried, that's all. I'm worried sick about what everyone is going to say."

"Say about what, Sis?"

"What is everyone going to say about BigHorn's hole?" Wringing my hands together, I say, "The rodeo is in three weeks, and I'm riding Rocky for sure, but I can't seem to get any sleep because I'm so scared Dad is going to find out about BigHorn. I want to come clean and tell him about it before he sees us riding him there."

Jackson shrugs. "I bet Dad already knows."

"I don't know how he would. Come on, it's getting cold." Hesitating for a single breath at the top of the steps, I exhale and push into the warm house.

Jackson follows me through the house mumbling something about horses and roping. We come into the kitchen as Mom and Dad are clearing their plates from the table. Relieved to be ending a two-week-old lie, I say, "Dad, I need to tell you that we plan, Jackson plans, to ride BigHorn over at Coach Phillip's place. That's why I never found him a new home." Chewing my lower lip, I add, "Sorry I didn't tell you sooner."'

Dad sits back in his chair, drumming his fingers across the top of the table. He says, "I figured, Cheyanna, but I still don't think it's a good idea, and I think Coach will back me up on that. Maybe the two of you should come with me to visit him tomorrow." Dad bends down and hoists little Cora onto his lap. "I spoke with Coach on the phone this morning. He's grateful for you kids feeding his animals and taking care of his place, and he wants to hear more about your rodeo projects."

He sits there bouncing Cora on his knee. I stare at him in surprise. I want to ask him how he knows, but I don't.

"Sure, Dad, we'd love to visit him. Actually, I think Coach will like BigHorn." Jackson's eyes grow wide with excitement as he says, "I do plan on keeping BigHorn as my roping horse, and I don't care what anybody thinks. He has an incredible ability to stop. I want to rope on him at the Ralston rodeo next month. But don't worry, Dad, Cheyanna is going to get old Rocky in shape, aren't you, Sis?"

I smile and nod at Jackson, grateful for this reminder that Rocky is not for sale. But I can't look Dad in the eye, because I've got mixed feelings about riding BigHorn, and I know he would disapprove if I chose him. I wish I was like Jackson; I wish I didn't care what people thought of me. BigHorn is such a beautiful horse, yet I can't imagine my friends seeing me on top of a horse with a hole in his neck. My head down, I escape to hide in my room. I can still hear Jackson and Dad's chatter.

"Well, I guess it's good that you don't want Yeller, Jackson," Dad chuckles. "Because that little fart has adopted me. He'd crawl into my pocket if he could."

Coach Phillip has been recuperating at the Washakie Hospital for the past two weeks. "Luck" is what the doctors are calling his recovery. "Mr. Phillip is lucky for surviving a broken pelvis and four cracked vertebrae," the doctors say. He is going to walk again soon. The doctors see no permanent damage to his spine. Coach is blessed.

We leave for the hospital after lunch. Dad's old Ford smells like warm mud and wet hay. I like riding in the car with Dad because we both enjoy country music, unlike Mom, who only listens to ancient rock 'n' roll.

Dad muffles a cough with the back of his hand and asks us, "What do the two of you plan to tell Mr. Phillip about the refugee you've stowed away at his place? Have you discussed what you'll say?"

I pretend not to hear him for a full minute, waiting for Jackson to answer. I'm watching the captivating fence posts flash by when Jackson finally says, "Dad, we'll ask Coach for advice with BigHorn. You know, how he would care for him, whether he would use him on the ranch or in competition, or both. That sort of thing." Jackson watches me in the rearview mirror. Smiling, he says, "Don't worry, Dad. I'll play it cool." Jackson looks over his shoulder at me and adds, "Not to mention, Coach is always happy to keep the team's horses."

I couldn't have said it better.

When we arrive at the hospital, a breeze rushes from the mouth of the nearby canyon. Grabbing my jacket, I run to the hospital entrance, excited to see Coach and eager to get into the warmth of the building. Once

I pass the automatic doors I hesitate; the building is too bright. The stagnant air smells of harsh chemicals, and it seems as if no window has been opened for countless decades. I stop to wait near the entrance. The door swooshes open as Dad and Jackson march in out of the wind.

We stand together, gathering our bearings. The lobby is busy with foot traffic. People wait, watching outside as the spring winds howl their serenade to the closing of winter. No one in the lobby rushes back into the raging winds without good reason.

The receptionist offers us a smile and directions. We gratefully accept and take the nearest elevator to the third floor. Walking through the broad corridor, I grab Jackson's arm and say, "I wish we'd thought to bring him something." We reach his room as a nurse is walking out.

"Is he awake?" Dad asks, smiling at the tiny man.

"You are his rodeo kids, I presume? You're all that he talks about." He puckers his lips, sighs, and says, "I just gave him his pain meds. I shouldn't let you go in there. He needs his rest." When we don't leave, he sighs again, "Alright. You can go see Mr. Phillip. Holler if he needs anything. And don't stay too long!" He wrinkles his nose and mumbles as he walks into the neighboring room.

Dad quietly pushes the door to Coach's room open and we slip in. The curtains are closed to any outside light and the blinking of the IV pump is the only movement in the room.

"Hi, Coach, how are you today?" Jackson asks as he

rushes to the bed and sits in the only chair. "We've been worried about you."

"Hi, Jackson. I'm so glad to see you kids," Coach says as he adjusts the oxygen tubing in his nose. "I hate to imagine where I would be today if it hadn't been for the two of you riding to my house. Thank you for helping me."

I stand beside Jackson's chair and ask, "How do you feel? "

"Well," Coach pauses and exhales through puffed cheeks. "I've had better days. The docs say that in addition to a concussion, I've got a broken pelvis and a couple of cracked vertebrae. Other than that, I'm snazzy!" Coach grimaces and says, "They say that if I

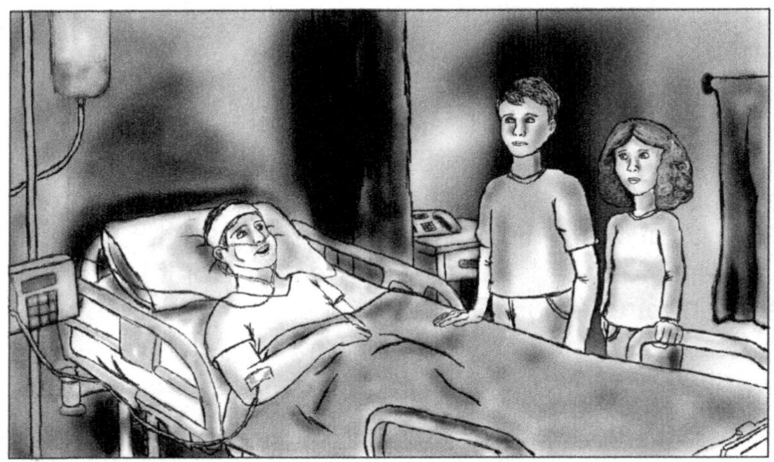

had moved while I was lying out there in the dirt, I would have never walked again. Fortunately, I kept passing out from the pain. So I'm mending, thanks to got me away from my wild colt. A few times, lying there in the dirt, that colt came too close to stomping on me. I thought he was going to finish the job of killing me."

"We were so afraid when we found you, Coach. I've never been so afraid," I say. Biting my lips, I scan the room for a trash can. The queasiness comes suddenly; my insides roll and slosh. I pace the floor beside the mobile bed, fighting the nauseating smells in the air.

Jackson, oblivious of my condition, says, "We can hardly wait to show you our new horses. We're going to work in your arena this spring. I'm taking Cheyanna's barrel racing horse." He stands and slaps me on the back. When he sees my face, however, Jackson stops smiling. "Sis, you okay? Here, Cheyanna, have my chair." Jackson pushes his chair toward me and walks to the sink. He brings me a cup of water with a small smile.

"Thanks, Jackson. That helps. I don't know how you can stand this place, Coach. I'd be climbing out the window if I had to be holed up in here," I say, sipping from the thick Styrofoam.

Dad stands in the corner, listening to our chatter. Finally, he interrupts, saying, "Eugene, I want to discuss the rodeo team with you."

Jackson and I exchange confused glances. We don't know what Dad is talking about or, for a moment, who he's talking to. We are always surprised when Dad calls Coach "Eugene"; he's always been "Coach" to us.

"Eugene, I would like to take over as the kid's rodeo coach for a while, until you're healed. You know, to keep things safe at the arena," Dad says.

"Sounds like a plan, Joe. Now, Jackson, tell me about this horse," Coach says, rubbing his hands together.

"I remember parts of what you kids told me in the round-pen that day, but some things are fuzzy. I'm not sure I remember the facts."

"Well, Coach, we call him BigHorn, but his full name is BigHornCatchMeQuick. Mom bought him for Cheyanna to barrel race. He's a runner. You'll see. He's big and long-legged, and can stop on a dime." Jackson takes a deep breath and looks in Dad's direction for an instant before saying, "He's also got a tracheotomy below his jaw."

I glance up—Coach is looking at me. "Now I remember what you told me when you found me. Here I thought I'd gone bonkers and dreamt all of this, but it's true. So, Cheyanna, this is why you're not running him?" Coach asks, not letting me escape his gaze. "Because of his trachea?"

"Jackson wants to rope on BigHorn, and my old Rocky has one more year of racing in him. I just need to get him in better condition," I reason, avoiding the question.

Coach's glance shifts toward my Dad and then back to me. Finally, Coach Phillip says, "Cheyanna, one day you will learn that it doesn't matter what others think or say about you or your horse." Coach pauses. Licking his lips, he adds, "I can't force that day to come, though, so you go ahead and get old Rocky in shape and running fast, and I'll be at your first rodeo cheering you on. Of course, you kids can use my ranch for whatever training you need. Now, I had better close my eyes and get some rest." Coach closes his eyes and says, "My pain pills are kicking in, and I'd hate to fall asleep while you're telling more news."

Coach starts to nod off as we say good-bye. We begin to file out of the room when Coach gently grabs my wrist. "I remember almost everything you told me, Cheyanna. You kids should both ride that horse. You both want to, and I heard that horse loves to run."

We all stop. Coach's words are mumbled and slurred, but I can hear the determination in his voice as he fights to remain conscious. "Cheyanna, you need to race for you. Not for anyone else. In doing that, you'll always be a winner." Then Coach's head falls to rest against the pillow and his eyes close.

I pull my hand away. Coach is now oblivious to my presence. I arrange the covers over him as I had done the day we found him in the dirt, recalling my confessions of fearing the crowds. Dad says, "Come on, Cheyanna, let him rest."

The drive home seems fast and Coach's words ring in my ears. The wind is quiet for the first time all day. Dad slows the big truck and switches off the radio. He leans over the back seat and says, "Cheyanna, Mr. Phillip was drugged and loopy today. Never mind whatever he said about you both riding BigHorn. I'm the coach now." He turns back towards the steering wheel and speeds home, saying, "You'll get Rocky conditioned over the next few weeks."

Parking the truck at the barn, we climb out to begin the evening chores. I glance at the magenta-streaked western sky, ridged with snow-capped peaks of purple and blue. The sky would look beautiful if I weren't so mad. I slam the truck's door as hard as my strength allows and stride off to do my chores. Rocky is already in good condition. And no, I will not "never mind" Coach.

In the days following our visit to the hospital, Coach's words constantly replay in my head: "You need to race for you." I think about them while Rocky and I ride the hills. Climbing the steep slopes makes Rocky stronger, and every day after dinner, I ride him to the Thunderbird Ranch arena. Rocky, now running faster than ever, is ready for the Ralston rodeo. Aside from stamina exercises, he's running the barrel racing pattern consistently, flawlessly, and mostly on autopilot. I realize, as I ride home in the rain from Coach Phillip's, that Rocky would be a perfect horse for my sister Cora. The weeks tick slowly by; my enthusiasm begins to dim when all I hear about is BigHorn and Jackson's impressive roping times.

Roping practice for the team is being held at Jackson's friend Steve's house. Steve's dad has fresh young roping calves and hay for their healthy appetites. Jackson has kept BigHorn at Steve's with all the other ropers for training. Dad, as my coach, concocts this grand scheme to have the roping practice separate from our barrel racing at Coach's place. Dad says, "This way we have more time and focus." I think Dad is doing this on purpose so that I don't get to see BigHorn. Maybe he thinks I'll change my mind if the red horse is out of my sight.

Chapter 8
Hugo

The rains finally stop, and the birds singing outside my window wake me before the sun comes up. I pull on my favorite sweatshirt and head outside to listen to the morning.

"Did the birds wake you up too?" Mom asks when I latch the screen door shut quietly.

"Morning, Mom. I thought I'd find you here; you love this quiet time of day."

"Come and sit with me, Cheyanna," she invites. "It looks like we'll finally have some sunshine, doesn't it?" Mom stands quickly to make room for me on the rocking bench, sloshing her coffee on the pine deck.

"Oh, I hope so. Rocky and I have nearly grown flippers." I mop up her coffee spills with my sleeve before sitting down.

The birds continue their endless chatter. It barely resembles song now, more like passionate chirplike conversation.

"I'm glad you got up to join me out here. Remember when we would sit here when you were small and watch the sunrise?" Mom rocks the bench ever so softly with her foot.

"Yeah, I love it out here. Those are some of my best memories," I reminisce.

"Yes, good memories," Mom agrees.

We sit and rock on the bench swing, both lost in thought.

Mom stops the swing with her toe and turns to me, saying, "Cheyanna, did you know that when I was twenty I ran, and won, on the county's ugliest horse?" She takes a deep breath and continues, "You must know that his ugliness didn't make him any slower, or any less lovely.

"Hugo was his name. He was Gramps' horse and was missing part of one ear, and patches of mane. He had white scars all over his face and neck. Gramps said he had a run-in with a mountain lion. I don't know if that was true, but he was a powerful horse. And man could he run. Folks would tease me and say that he was only fast because he was scared of himself and was trying to get away."

Mom takes a big breath. "But I loved that horse. Hugo worked so hard and at the end of the day when the racing was over, he would sidle up to me and plant wet kisses all over my face. He won any rodeo I raced him in, and better yet, he loved every second of it."

I listen to Mom and to the birds as she gently pumps the swing again. "It doesn't matter what your horse looks like, Chey. What matters is that your horse is fast, and that you understand one another. Rodeo is a competition, a test of your relationship," she says.

We both look up as the birds stop their ruckus. A quiet settles around us as she looks toward me again. "Rodeo is for the thrill and the fun; the crowds mean nothing. Winning is the best feeling, and I just want you to experience that." Mom pats me gently on the back, stands up, and goes into the house, leaving me with her words.

The quiet encroaches. Not a ruffle in the trees nor the grass breaks my thoughts until suddenly the wind picks up. The wind seems to blow straight down from the mountain and starts without warning. I jump to my feet and race across the deck to the front door. Dad sits at the kitchen table reading a newspaper and drinking coffee. "Morning, sunshine. Did the wind blow you in just like it blew the birds away?" he asks.

"No, the birds are still out there, but yes, the wind did blow me in."

"Are you hungry? I'll make some pancakes." Dad gets up and sets the skillet on the stove before I can even agree. I get a bowl and head to the refrigerator for some eggs. We work together in the stillness of the kitchen, listening to the wind rage outside.

"Should I wake Cora and Jackson?" I ask.

"Nah, let them sleep. If they're hungry, the smell of food will wake them." Dad takes a stack of plates from the cupboard. We each take one and pile it with hotcakes. Well, Dad does. Me, I can eat only one.

Sitting at the table, I ask, "Did you know Mom when she ran her horse Hugo at the rodeos?"

Dad smiles and leans back in his chair. "Yup, I did. He was faster than my old truck. I know because she raced me," he laughs.

"Was he ugly?"

"Ugly? Well..." Dad scratches his chin. "I guess I never thought about Hugo's looks, but as a matter of fact, yeah, he was ugly. Really ugly." Dad stabs a bite of pancake with his fork.

"Him being ugly didn't matter, though, did it? You said that you didn't even remember him being that way," I point out.

Dad sets his fork down. He knows where our conversation is leading. "Cheyanna," he says. "When I was your age I would get in fights at school, then I would get in trouble. Big trouble." Dad leans closer to me. "People, kids especially, can be mean simply because they don't know any better. When someone or something is not like everyone else, they will make fun, tease, and pick on you."

The wind bursts through the kitchen with Francis close behind. "Morning, family!" he shouts over the wind that lingers in our ears. Sport whimpers his good morning too and lies at Francis' feet.

"Do you have a panni-cake for the Francis?" he asks as he helps himself.

"Good morning, Francis. Of course, come have some breakfast, " Dad says with a smile.

"What you two talking 'bout?" he asks, tossing Sport a piece of his pancake

"I was telling Cheyanna about how people can be mean when someone is different."

"Oh, I see," Francis nods. "You tell Chey about yours fights you helped me to win when all them kids would gang up on me? Francis little brother be Francis hero." He gives Dad his shy smile.

I poke at my pancake; it suddenly doesn't taste as good as before. Looking to Dad with a new understanding, I say, "I don't care if people are mean about BigHorn."

"You right, Chey." Francis speaks with his mouth full. "People are mean, you might win or you won't. All's that's matters then is you. How you feel here." Francis thumbs his chest.

Dad looks at me, his face suddenly stern. "You're just saying that because you've never experienced it. And I won't let you go through that. End of story. Now let's eat in peace."

Chapter 9
Rocky's Last Rodeo

A few weeks later, the first rodeo of the season arrives. The sun burns red, reflecting off the sand in the arena. "I could use some shades today," I mutter, licking my chapped lips. My stomach is in knots; there is no saliva in my mouth to spit. My hands are moist from nerves. A breeze gusting down from the mountain doesn't do much to relieve the heat.

"This is your last run, Rocky. We've worked hard for this, old boy." Rocky raises his head and snorts. He's ready. I quietly talk to him as we ride to the arena's open gate. "Come on, boy, let's make Mom and Dad proud." Inside, though, my heart feels as if it will leap from my chest. I can feel the collective gaze of everyone in the grandstand penetrate my skin.

Remembering how perfectly Rocky can race the pattern, I close my eyes. I touch his flank with the tip of my spurs. Flecks of sand kick up and sting my face. The cool air blows hard against me in our sudden speed as we dash across the arena. I tense my shoulders as we near the first barrel, racing the clock. "Run, Rocky! Run!" I shout over the roar of his clattering hooves and cheers from the fence.

Time stands still. My world is just the horse beneath me. I sink back into the saddle, ready for our second turn. Pressing my spur firmly into his left side, I coax Rocky to bend around the barrel. Looking ahead to the third can, I drive him hard to the upcoming turn. This one has our name on it. "We've got it!" Sweat streams down my forehead and stings my eyes as we finish the race. Rocky slows as we come through the arena's gate, and I'm trembling like a brittle leaf in a windstorm.

The drama and adrenaline fade in the heat of the springtime air. Rocky's belly rises and falls beneath the saddle. My jeans, damp with sweat, stick to my skin too snugly for my liking. I know that Rocky needs to cool down and move around slowly for a while before he is allowed to have that drink he surely craves, or he'll risk having a bellyache.

"Come on, Rock, that was a good run."

My heart drums uncontrollably. The crowd roars in applause. I lick my lips again, tasting the dirt from the arena floor. I like not knowing my race time just yet. Rocky and I have never once felt a victory in the two years that we've raced. I have a feeling this, our first contest of the season, is our fastest one yet. I smile. It's over. I clamber down from the saddle. Loosening the cinch on Rocky's belly, we walk toward the overflowing water tank. I eagerly help myself to a cool, sweet drink from the spigot before shutting the valve off. Waiting for Rocky to get his fill, I hear Dad's voice hollering from the direction of the arena.

"That was your best run ever, Cheyanna! You two did marvelously!"

Searching in the direction of his voice, I take off my hat and hold it to shade my eyes. I find Dad's red shirt in the crowd. He's leaning against the fence and balancing Cora on the top rail with Mom standing at his side. "Hey, you three," I holler. They wave at me and little Cora gives me a thumbs-up.

Smiling inwardly, I say to Rocky, "Hold on, Rock. That'll do for now." I gently lift his head away from the tank and lead him to the arena fence where Dad and Cora wait. Right then, I see my friend Jasmine's silver-plated bridle shimmer from the starting gate.

Jasmine's run is over in a blink. A few contestants later, an announcement crackles from the aged speaker atop the lamppost. A woman's husky voice rattles off the final times of the many barrel racers: "Our top five cowgirls today, beginning with Cheyanna Ashley's run of 18.02, brings her trailing in fifth place."The husky voice continues. Dad wraps his arm around my waist and pulls me close.

"See?" he says. "I knew you could make a barrel horse out of your old cow-pony. All it took was some hard work." Dad gives me a tighter squeeze.

"I'm sure I would have done better on BigHorn."

The smile on Dad's face disappears.

"Eighteen point zero two seconds? Wow, that was your fastest time!" Mom interrupts before Dad has a chance to argue.

"I'm so proud of you!" Mom continues to shout. "You ran your best run today. I know that you didn't win, but I'm proud of you for working so hard with Rocky." She looks toward Rocky, studying him from nose to tail.

"We placed! I'm proud of that too, Mom!" I smile, ignoring the blank expression on Dad's face. The run today felt good. Resting my boot on the bottom arena pole, I scrape muck from the sole. Then I say, "I'm retiring Rocky today. He's getting too old for this."

Swallowing hard, I look up to make sure Dad is listening. He raises his eyebrows so I add, "I'm only retiring him from the junior rodeo. "

Smiling down at Cora, I scoop her up and set her in the saddle atop Rocky's back. "I'm going to give Rocky to Cora."

Cora grins. Holding tightly to the saddle horn, she reaches for the reins.

I hand them up to her and say, "You have to learn to stay awake while you're riding, though." I smile at my tiny sister sitting big in the saddle. "We'll work on that. I'll start taking you for short rides," I say as I put her down. She giggles and runs towards the stands and

Mom chases after her, leaving me alone with Dad.

Dad doesn't look at me. Kicking the loose gravel with his ragged boot, his eyes are focused downward. He clears his throat and says, "It wouldn't have mattered if you'd won on BigHorn. He's got a tracheotomy, Cheyanna. Even if he was fast enough, people would still talk and tease you. No one would cheer for you on that horse."

"I want to at least try to stick up for someone I love, Dad. I know BigHorn is an outstanding horse and I love him. I hope Jackson proves exactly how special he is today. BigHorn is my horse, and I do want to ride him." I pause for a moment, waiting for Dad to reply, but he doesn't. He's listening with his head cocked to one side. The furrow of his eyebrow doesn't change.

So I continue, "If you want the money for Rocky, I've got twelve hundred dollars in savings from the county fair. I am giving Rocky to Cora. She's ready for him, and he's ready for her." Out of breath, I drop my shoulders and unclench my fists in anticipation of Dad's reaction.

Dad takes one step closer. He takes hold of my shoulders and says, "It's not about the money." Dad crosses his arms and looks at me sternly. "I'm the parent and my decision on BigHorn is final. I told you to get him another home and you disobeyed me. Now Jackson is roping on him, which I'm not too happy about, but I know he can handle what people say. But I can't let you barrel race on that horse. I don't want you to be hurt."

I kick the dirt with my boots. "That's not fair! I can take it! I can convince people to love BigHorn despite his defect. Remember the story about Hugo?"

"You heard what I said, Cheyanna," Dad replies as he turns his back and walks away. I stroke Rocky with a shaking hand and head toward the truck and trailer, with tears beginning to well in my eyes.

I tie Rocky to the trailer, and gently unsaddle him. I wipe him down with a wet cloth and give him a small bite of grain, tears streaming down my face all the while. Deciding that a treat will lift my spirits, I search the truck for some money and walk to the concession stand.

With a Popsicle in hand, I turn to go wait at the truck and bump into Mom and Cora.

"Hey, I'm glad you found something cold. Can you believe how hot it's gotten today? What's wrong? Have you been crying?" Mom asks. I shake my head, but Mom doesn't look convinced. "Okay, if you say so. Come with me and we'll watch the roping," she responds. She holds Cora's hand and wraps her free arm over my slumped shoulders.

"I'll be right behind you two, Mom. I'd better go check on Rocky again. He might have kicked his water over or something," I say.

"No, I was just at the truck. He's fine." Despite the bright sun, Mom takes her sunglasses off and looks me in the eyes. "Come and watch Jackson with everyone."

I sigh. I want to watch Jackson, but I don't want to watch BigHorn when I know he'll never be mine. Feeling a lump in the back of my throat, I look away.

Mom misinterprets my feelings. "Oh," Mom says. "I know you and your dad are hoping to find another

horse, one that would be more popular with the crowds. I just wish you two would give BigHorn a chance." Mom places her shades back on her face and puts her hands on her hips. "Jackson rides in an hour. I hope to see you there."

"Mom, I actually want to ride BigHorn. I've been thinking a lot about what you said to me. You've given me the courage. BigHorn is my Hugo." Mom's face breaks into a smile and she hugs me to her chest.

"I'm so proud of you, Chey, you've really grown up. I admire how strong you've become."

I try to smile, but I can't lift the corners of my mouth. "I'm just afraid Dad is never going to let me ride him."

Mom puts her hand on my cheek. "We'll try to work something out."

"Sure, Mom, good luck with that." I say glumly. I stuff my hands deep into the pockets of my jeans. "I'll be over in a while, save me a seat," I holler over my shoulder as I walk towards the truck.

At least Mom is on my side, but what can she do? Dad is really stubborn. My head begins to pound in rhythm with my heart, and I'm relieved Dad is not around. I find a bit of hot shade beside my oldest friend, Rocky, and lie down in the dirt to rest. Rocky swings his massive head over me and snorts into my hair, making me smile a little.

From my spot of shade, I listen to the roars from the bleachers around the arena. Alone with my thoughts and worries, I fight the urge to sleep. I replay the events of the past month over in my mind. My quest to discover the dream horse is now a family drama. The horse found for me has become my brother's rope horse, one that Dad is ashamed to have me ride. Mom and I are stuck with desperately trying to get Dad to change his mind.

I close my eyes against the bright sun and my ears to the hum of the grandstand. Breathing slowly, I calm my raging mind and slowly relax. "I'll only sleep for a minute, Rocky," I say sleepily. "Maybe when I wake up, the roping will be over. I bet Jackson will win today."

I drift off to dream.

Dad races BigHorn around the barrels. Smiling, he says, "Touch the horse's shoulder gently right before going into each turn, keep your leg solid in the stirrup, and give him something to bend around, Cheyanna. He's fast and fun to ride! Please race him. I know you'll love him. Everyone will."

Hovering on the brink of my dream, I smile.

BigHorn leaps into a sprint around the empty arena. He and Dad gallop toward me, throwing sand through the air. I see Dad's smile, and it's bigger than it's ever been. He slides to a stop and flecks of sand sprinkle across my face, disrupting my dreamy state.

"Wake up, Cheyanna," I hear my friend Jasmine say. She kicks my boot once, then a second time with a bit more gusto, peppering my bare skin with pebbles.

I can't remember a time in my childhood that Jasmine wasn't my best friend. Like most friends, we share a lot of interests, and horses are no exception. In grade school, Jasmine and I spent countless days in the saddle exploring the ranch or racing in the meadow. As we have grown, our competitiveness has grown too. We are rivals when it comes to barrel racing, but we don't let it come between our friendship.

"Wake up, you lazy bum, you're going to miss Jackson's roping!" Jasmine says.

Awake and confused, I jump up and brush dust off the seat of my jeans. Smiling at my old friend, I ask, "What time is it? I didn't mean to fall asleep but I was having such a lovely dream." I don't wait for a reply before reaching over the hot truck bed in search of the cooler and something to drink. Jasmine reaches in too.

"Coach Phillip sent me to find you."

"Oh wow, he's here?" I ask.

"Yes, they discharged him last night. He said he's so excited to be here to see you and Jackson. He wants me to make sure you watch Jackson rope. Have you been asleep all this time? I wondered why you didn't find me after my run. You and Rocky did great, you know." Jasmine chooses a cola and pulls her hand from the cooler.

"Yeah, thanks, today's time was our fastest ever," I reply, dazed by my strange dream. Shaking my head, I come back to reality and ask Jasmine, "What time did you run?"

"Seventeen seconds flat! I placed third." Jasmine responds with a grin. "Now, come on. I'm glad I found you. We'd better get over to the arena before your brother ropes. I sure as heck don't want to miss him."

"Now, why is that?" I ask. Jasmine has never shown this much interest in my brother before.

She just giggles and walks ahead.

"Whatever," I say as I crack open my soda and take a long gulp.

Jackson is the last cowboy to rope. We make it to the seats Mom and Cora have saved us with more than enough time to sit and bake in the hot spring sun. The husky woman's voice rattles over the speaker, interrupting my fretting. "Jackson Ashley is our final roper in the boy's breakaway roping today. Jackson, you're up."

The steer is put into the roping chute. Jackson smoothly backs BigHorn into the roping box next to the calf. His arm behind him and his silver hat pulled down, he tips his head. The calf bursts out in search of its mother.

BigHorn jumps from the roping box, and in one lightning motion he is close on the calf's heels. With sudden speed and a massive stride, the great animal is above the black calf and in position for Jackson to

rope. Jackson swings his rope over his head once, then throws his loop around the calf's neck. BigHorn shuts down in a flash; his front legs stiffen, outstretched in front of his large frame, and his rump dips low to the arena floor.

The calf hits the end of the rope. Jackson's rope breaks free, just as it's meant to do in breakaway roping, and no flags are called by the judges; he had a clean run, and BigHorn didn't chase after the calf too soon. Jackson rides to the far end of the arena behind the little lone calf, encouraging it into the open pen. We watch as Jackson retrieves his lariat and rides back along our side of the fence. He stops below us, smiling. "Good ride!" Jasmine yells before I can say a word.

Jackson smirks at me, Jasmine, Mom, and Cora before riding out of the arena toward Coach, who sits in his wheelchair at the base of the stadium. When we get up to follow, I notice Dad is pushing Coach's wheelchair.

Outside the arena, we find Jackson standing beside BigHorn at the water tank. "Don't let him drink too much too fast," I advise when he notices me watching.

"Will do, Coach Cheyanna," he says with a grin. Threading the rein through his fingers, Jackson looks at Jasmine while speaking to me.

Before I could respond, Jasmine says to Jackson, "It must take so much practice to be able to rope the cow so quickly. You did so great out there."

Jackson, turning away from me, says, "Oh, it's nothing, Jazz. You know I've been roping since I was eight; it's no big deal to a pro like me."

"So you're a pro huh?" Jasmine grins as Jackson continues listing off his roping accomplishments. I roll my eyes and leave the two lovebirds to their conversation. I doubt they even realize I left.

Chapter 10
I Quit

Jackson's endless bragging about his big win fuels my frustration as we begin our drive home. We are all proud of his win, but I am sick of hearing about it over and over and over again. Watching the starlit night slip by outside the truck's window, I fall into a trance listening to Jackson's boasting.

Thinking out loud, I say, "Rodeo isn't only about the winning."

"What did you say, Chey?" Jackson asks.

"Rodeo. It's not just about the winning because if it is, then I'm doing it all wrong. I could learn to like it, get used to the crowds, maybe?" I mutter to myself. I need to stop caring what they think.

Jackson apparently doesn't hear me and replies with, "Yeah, BigHorn is an amazing horse. He's calm in the box, stops on a dime, and loves to run. That's the thing, Cheyanna. He loves to run and wants to run, too." Jackson lets out a big sigh, tosses his head back and says, "I'm glad you're finally going to run him on the barrels."

"Who said Cheyanna was going to run BigHorn on the barrels?" Dad asks. He reaches down and shuts the radio off.

"I guess I did," Jackson says. "That is, if you don't mind me roping on him now and then?" he turns and asks me.

"Dad is worried that people will be mean and tease me about BigHorn, Jackson."

"Well, if anyone is mean, I'll pop him in the nose." Jackson slams his fist into his hand.

"Okay now, Jackson." Dad slows the truck down. "That is exactly why Chey is not riding BigHorn. I'm not having my kids getting in fights, especially not fights over a horse. I will not have Cheyanna be the center of everyone's jokes."

An hour of silence passes before Cora speaks. "We go for a ride tomorrow?" she asks.

"Maybe not tomorrow, Bug. I'm tired from the rodeo today. The day after, I promise," I say.

The silent drive goes on forever. I go back to my stargazing out the window and realize that when push comes to shove I ***will*** fight other kids for BigHorn in order to protect him. I am more like Dad than I ever thought.

I'm suddenly reminded of Francis and what he said the other morning about how I feel in my heart. "How do I feel here?" I ask myself, holding my hand to my chest.

"Dad," I say, breaking the silence and waking Jackson and Cora.

"What's up, Chey?" he asks.

"Dad, if you won't let me stick up for BigHorn, then I just won't rodeo."

I can see Dad's eyes widen with shock in the rearview mirror.

Mom turns around, catches my gaze, and gives me the faintest of smiles as she asks Dad, "Why did you get into trouble with your parents when you fought with other kids?" She rubs Dad's shoulder with her left hand. "Did you not tell your folks that you were sticking up for Francis?" Mom swings her arm over the back of the truck's seat. "Fighting is wrong when there's no call for it. You're right about that, Joe. But standing up for yourself or someone you love? That's hard to do sometimes, but standing up for another shows what a good person you are."

The truck falls quiet after that, but I can see Dad's body remain tense behind the wheel for the rest of the drive. We arrive home with a full moon coming over the canyon rim. I can smell rain nearby. Jackson leads Big Horn, and I lead Rocky to the pasture gate. The walk feels good after the long drive cramped in the backseat of the truck. The silence between us as we walk the horses to the field is welcomed. I can feel a headache setting in and I don't want to discuss rodeo or BigHorn for another million years.

Chapter 11
BigHorn to the Rescue

A pale morning glow rests on the canyon ridge when I roll over and peek out my window. Jumping from the bed, I feel the undeniable need to get away from the tension of last night. I fumble in the dark for my cowboy boots and leather gloves. I know that it will be cool from last night's rain, so I pull my wool sweater over my head.

The air feels damp and tastes sweet. The light above the barn door is still on. My eyes adjust to the dark morning as the eastern horizon turns crimson. Alone, I walk back to the pasture gate where Jackson and I put the horses out the night before.

Gently rattling my small grain bucket, I coax both Rocky and BigHorn back to the gate. I ease the halter over Rocky's head and hold the gate upright with my shoulder to keep BigHorn from following us out. BigHorn willingly backs away from the gate, but a few feet away, he twirls and trots in circles. I remember that he can't nicker or neigh, but he is trying to tell me something. Rocky understands, though, because he stops just past the gate and refuses to leave his new friend. With a snort and grunt, Rocky covers my sweater in his pleading slobber. "Well, well, well, your buddy wants to come along and see some country? We can show him our favorite places. Maybe we'll get to know him better." Dropping the gate open, I let both horses follow me to the barn.

I brush and saddle Rocky while he nibbles his grain. "We make a perfect team, you and I, Rock. I promise that you'll always be my horse even if you're not my barrel horse. I'll never let anyone but Cora take you." I slip a halter over BigHorn's head as soon as he's done with his snack. "And you, BigHorn, I won't rodeo on any horse but you. So I suppose I just won't rodeo at all." I climb into the saddle atop Rocky, and leading BigHorn, we head up the dirt road. The sun rises higher, leaving the canyon rim.

We ride along, listening to the morning come alive. A coyote yips from a nearby ridge. "You scaredy-cat," I holler. My horses prance and stomp with excitement at the sound. "His bark is worse than his bite, you two. He's too afraid of us to show his face."

Trotting along the trail, the two horses settle down as we continue. Many other animal noises fill the air. The chatter of sage grouse is amusing as they spook from their water pool; they sound like mice arguing over a block of cheese. "Are you two ready for a drink?" We stop at the creek beneath a juniper tree. I jump from my saddle, sending BigHorn into a startled leap. "Whoa, big guy," I say, calming him down. I bend down to drink, and the water is almost too icy to swallow. I take a couple of small sips to quench my thirst.

Holding both my reins and BigHorn's lead rope, I sit watching the two horses drinking from the mountain stream. I examine BigHorn's trachea more closely than before. Four, maybe five inches long, the stoma opens across the width of his trachea, exposing pink flesh and the pale cartilage rings of the windpipe.

"BigHorn, you don't have trouble at all, do you? I heard you take a big gulp of air back there when you spooked." I run my fingers through his mane. "Just like any other horse... and yet Dad can't accept you." BigHorn lifts his head from the water and presses his wet muzzle into my chest. The hole looks kind of drippy, though. Jackson told me that the hole draining like this was normal. "I guess it's like a normal horse's boogers." I smile. "Let's get going, boys, or we'll miss Mom's breakfast."

I climb back into the saddle and we ride down the wet and slick trail. I pull BigHorn up beside me and slip his halter from his nose. "You don't need that anymore, boy. You need to be able to see your footing." After I tie the loose rope around my saddle horn, we continue down the path.

Lost in the quiet morning, I find peace for the first time since BigHorn came to live with us. BigHorn, happy to be free of the halter, takes bite after bite of mountain grass along the trail. Without warning, a low grumble from my empty stomach causes both horses to raise their heads and perk their ears.

"That was just me, boys." I reassure them. "I could almost get down and eat some of that grass with you. We'd better get home. Let's go on down to the reservoir and look around for stray bulls. That's the first thing Dad will ask me about this morning. Then we'll head back along the road by the river."

Rocky softly exhales with a grunt as if to say, "Let's go, I'm game." BigHorn obediently tags along with perked ears, as if adding, "Sure, I don't have anything better to do this morning."

A distressed bawl shatters the silence.

"Listen, boys. You hear that?"

I straighten in the saddle, trying to get a better earful of the frantic sound again. I watch the horses' ears for clues of trouble as we pick our way down the grassy slope. The horses must hear it too, because they walk with their heads raised and ears turned forward. I can feel the thumping rhythm of my racing heart in my chest. There it is! There's a splashing and gurgling sound coming from the reservoir.

"Oh, no!"

Something is down in the water!

"Giddy up, Rock!" I holler and tap Rocky's belly with my spurs. We charge down the trail as I grab a tighter hold on the reins. The two horses and I no longer proceed out of curiosity alone. Adrenaline propels us to the rescue. It's a drowning cow, a nightmare come true. What can I possibly do alone?

We trot into the open prairie surrounding the small lake. I see the reservoir ahead, yet it seems far. A dark figure fights to keep its nose above the surface of the murky water. Thrashing about, the animal works itself into a deeper part of the reservoir. I see it jerk its head up as its nose skims the surface. The animal's strength must be fading. We gallop to the shore.

"Haw, Rocky!" We stop at the water's edge. Here, from the back of my horse, I see the horror of the situation. A muddy and tired bull raises his massive skull to inspect his visitors. He shakes his weary head from side to side despairingly. "Whoa now, big fella," I say, wiping a sweaty palm across my jeans. "At least you have some spunk in you. With you still wanting to fight like that, maybe we can get you out of there."

I see the purple tag in his right ear: Traveler929. It's Dad's prize bull. "We need to act fast, boys," I say, glancing around for anything we can use to leverage the huge bull ashore. "We have to try."

A lone tree stands at the edge of the pond, its stout trunk emerging from the black mud. BigHorn is peacefully grazing up the hillside.

I untie BigHorn's halter from the saddle and trot toward him on Rocky. "We're going to need your help here too, BigHorn." He lowers his head to my belly as I place the halter over his ears. I climb back in the saddle and lead him back to the water's edge.

I watch as the bull closes his eyes and lowers his black nose to the water's surface once more. Bubbles startle him awake as he jerks his head out of the water again.

The poor thing might have been here all night. "We've got to get a rope on him. We can try to spook him out, Rocky, but I don't want you getting bogged down with him." I tie BigHorn's rope to the tree so he doesn't wander and in case I need to get to him in a hurry.

Rocky and I trot to the opposite side of the pond and come toward the bull from behind. I yell, "Whoop, ya! Big guy! Gee up! Psst!" The bull raises his head and gives us a good snort but otherwise doesn't react. "This isn't going to get him out, Rock. He's pooped. Let's go back to the tree."

We come toward him from the front. Trotting back to the tree, I take my lariat off the saddle horn. The bull lifts his head again and watches us approach. We slow to a tiptoe and creep past the water's edge. "Careful now, that's close enough!" I raise my loop and swing once, then twice, and throw a loop that rests around his head. I pull out the extra slack and watch as the bull tosses his head from side to side and bellows. "We've made him angry!" I gasp. Rocky and I maneuver our way backward and out of the muddy water.

The bull has his legs under him, at least, and now he's got more fight in him, too. That's what he needs; more fight. He's not going to drown while we sit here and watch.

Rocky and I pull and tug on the rope to no effect. The bull only fights us, sinking further into the water and yanking the rope from my hand. Sitting in the saddle, I watch my rope bob to and fro in the reservoir. "It's around his neck, but now what are we going to do?" I ask my two steeds. They certainly want nothing to do with the big, wet bovine. Rocky strikes the water with his front hoof.

I sit thinking for too long and the bull's nose takes another dip beneath the water's surface. "Up, boy, hang on!" I holler. Hopping from the saddle, I trek out into the mud. Talking quietly to keep myself calm as much as the bull, I say, "I have a plan, big fellow. We're

going to get you out of this bog-hole, but I can't do it alone." Scanning the empty horizon, I see my only option. "We'll have to go back for help." Scooping up the loose end of my lasso, I quickly slop back through the muck toward my horse.

Back in the saddle and wet to my waist, I dally the rope around the saddle horn. The bull stares at me with wide eyes, but he doesn't fight against the rope's pressure. "Okay, boys, here's what we have to do," I say. "I don't see any way that we are going to pull that mammoth out of this mud without killing one of us. We have to keep his head up and out of the water while I get Dad."

Both horses are looking at the bull, not as concerned with the scene as I am. Rocky, trying to paw at the water a second time, gets a flick to his shoulder. "Cut that out, Rock. I need you to behave here," I scold.

Realizing that the rope could break with the bull's full weight, I fix my rope to the saddle horn. Then I untie BigHorn's lead from the tree and remove his halter.

"You had better stay close. We'll need to make a quick getaway," I say as I turn BigHorn free. He goes back to munching grass along the hillside.

The bull closes his eyes when I venture back into the murky pond. Hesitating a moment, I keep talking. "Give me a second, old boy. I've got to get this halter on you. That rope around your neck isn't going to do any of us any good when you fall asleep, is it?" I reach the drowning bull and put my left hand under water, holding the nosepiece of the halter. With one tug, I pull the fastened halter up and around his head. He jerks alert with a snort, knocking me backward into the water. Submerged and afraid, I scramble upright for air. On shore, Rocky holds tightly to the big bull. I leave the bull, grab the loose end of the rope, and run ashore.

Glad to be out of the water, I clamber to the lone tree, wet and cold, but determined. I shimmy as far up the tree as the rope will allow and tie a bowline to a large branch. My heart swells with pride and relief when I look down at my captive, his head raised from the water with the halter. Before easing out of the tree, I look around and spot my ride home. BigHorn's ears perk. He must know I am looking at him. I hope he doesn't suspect my plans. It's not easy to ride a horse bareback, but I didn't saddle or bridle him this morning.

"Don't you make a run for it, BigHorn," I say. "You're going to be my taxi home today." He still grazes along the hill's slope, unaware of the activities in the water below. Reluctant to leave poor Rocky bull-sitting at the reservoir, I pause beside the tree and curse, "What a great day to leave my cell phone." I doubt I'd have service here anyway. Sighing, I creep up the hillside.

Halfway up the slope, BigHorn stands watching the bull fighting in the water. Rocky keeps a steady tension on the rope between him and the bull. I hope that tension keeps the bull from putting too much weight on the poor tree. Something is eventually going to give way; I just hope I can get back before that happens.

At last, the bull settles into his sling and shuts his eyes. I close in on BigHorn and slip my arms around his neck. I imagine the moment BigHorn has any idea of what I'm up to, he will bolt. "Now for the hard part," I say, shutting my eyes and exhaling. "Easy, boy, stand still."

I scan for a rock to use for a leg up but not one rock is within my reach. I have to get aboard my mount before he gets a notion to leave. Without a moment to lose, I grab a handful of mane with my left fist. Standing with our shoulders touching, I swing my right leg up and over BigHorn's back with all my might. BigHorn startles and takes off in a gallop up the hillside. I can't help but grin as I clutch my fists in the horse's hair. I am finally riding my new horse; bareback, like a Native American on a wild stallion. For a moment, I cannot help but think of the Cheyenne Indians, my namesakes, wandering freely across the Great Plains, the wind in their long black hair.

"Settle down, BigHorn. We need to work together here." We ease into a smooth stride, headed home. I can tell by his laid back ears that he isn't used to this sort of entertainment, and neither am I. Both of my legs burn, but I hold on with all my might, squeezing even tighter with my tired knees. I dig my leg into his right flank. BigHorn begins to veer from the pressure and head toward the road and closer to our ranch. I urge the big horse to run faster. If something happens to Rocky, I'll never forgive myself. He could get into trouble by the reservoir; if the tree snaps, the bull might pull him in. I'm tempted, just for an instant, to turn back and untie the dallied horse from the bull.

"I don't think we could turn back now, BigHorn, even if I wanted to. I don't know how I'm going to stop you, let alone turn you."

I clutch his mane tighter. The more I squeeze with my legs around his belly, the faster the animal travels.

BigHorn's quick responses to my commands confirm that he is not only a superb athlete, but a smart and well-trained race horse.

Smiling, I gradually adapt to the motion of his flight. My anxieties over staying aboard subside.

Each stride of his long legs leaves yards of ground behind. I have to ignore the mud and pebbles that churn up and into my face. Fighting the urge to close my eyes and leap off, I let the big horse run as hard and fast as he will go. My hands are wet from sweat, and the cool wind whips my hair into a cyclone as we race for help.

I can feel the pulse of his drumming heart beneath me. We soar.

"I'm flying!" I scream and laugh into the air. BigHorn's mane dances in my face like smoke.

The freedom of this flight is like nothing I have ever experienced. I relax into BigHorn's stride and feel his muscles as they stretch and contract. I become one with his movements.

Looking up, I can finally see the approaching pasture fence. We made it in record time.

"Thanks for the lift home, Pegasus!" I laugh. Sitting up straighter, I lean back against his rump to cue him to a slower pace. The big horse reads my signal and slows, but we are still covering ground too rapidly. More conscious of the rocks and brush flying past, I tighten my grasp on his mane again.

"Do you mind slowing down some more?" I sink back. "Whoa, boy! We're coming up on that fence!"

I spot Dad standing by the barn, watching.

I shove my knees into BigHorn's sides and exhale gratefully when he comes to a smooth stop. I slip to the hard ground, and my legs wobble from sheer exhaustion. BigHorn stands beside me, watching me and waiting. His ribs heave, and the trachea beneath his chin is clean and pink. He reaches down for a taste of moist grass, swallowing big gulps of air through his throat.

Dad races towards us. "What's going on?" he shouts, his voice full of worry.

"A bull is down in the lower reservoir!" I gasp.

"Where's Rocky? Why did you ride BigHorn home?"

"We need the tractor," I reply, ignoring Dad's question. "I don't think the truck will pull him out."

Without another word, Dad turns and races back toward the tractor, leaving BigHorn alone on the gravel road.

Dad pulls the tractor up alongside me, and I jump in. Dad glances towards me, wipes his shirtsleeve across his face, and asks, "Why did you ride that horse back? And why were you riding bareback?"

I take several deep breaths as I watch the familiar scenery. My heartbeat begins to quiet, leaving me room to speak. "I left Rocky holding the bull's head out of the water, dallied to the saddle horn. The bull wouldn't fight anymore, and he kept falling asleep. We waited there at the reservoir a long time for the bull to give up and settle down. Dad, it's your Traveler bull. I hadn't saddled BigHorn so I was forced to ride him bareback."

Dad doesn't ask any more questions.

Approaching the grassy basin, I see the lone tree is still erect at the reservoir's edge. Then a dark figure of a horse appears, calmly standing and facing the water. "Thank you, God," I say, slapping my hands against my thighs. Finally, the reservoir is close enough that we see the bull. His head is held up and out of the water by the little tree, steadied by the horse holding the opposite end of the lariat that circles the bull's neck. What a sight they are, both waiting patiently for their rescuers to return!

Dad quickly approaches the water with the tractor and drives right up to Rocky. Rocky whinnies in delight. The exhausted bull lifts his head slightly and opens his eyes. Dad climbs down from the tractor, grinning.

"Good job, Chey. That's number 929. I paid a small fortune for that dude. Come on, let's get him out." Dad walks to Rocky and takes the rope down off his saddle horn.

I walk over and take Rocky's rein. Petting his forelock, I ask, "Can I unsaddle him and turn him free? He deserves some grass."

"Sure thing, Chey. He deserves more than grass, but that'll have to wait till he gets home." Dad walks to the tractor and pulls chains and a strap out of the back.

Dad sloshes through the water toward the bull. I hold my breath while he reaches under to secure the free end of a chain around the massive creature's feet. Not until Dad emerges from the water do I dare to exhale.

What feels like hours later, Dad climbs back on the tractor to hoist the poor bull from the lake. We're both soaked to the core with smelly black mud. The halter and rope remain around the bull's head as he rests on the banks of the reservoir. I creep close and retrieve my lariat and lead. Exhausted, the bull lowers his head to my touch.

Rocky trots too far ahead to catch, so I let him find his own way home. "He'll beat us, I bet," I say, shrugging and waving him off with a flip of my wrist.

Dad and I drive home along the river. The sun warms my muddy, wet clothes through the window. The surge of adrenaline drains from my blood and leaves me exhausted. I feel the need to shut my eyes as the tractor purrs slowly along. The warm sun feels welcoming and comfortable as I relax in the cozy old seat. I lean my head against Dad's shoulder and close my eyes.

Chapter 12
The Apology

The interruption of the engine's gentle roar disrupts my sleep. I sit up and stretch my arms out yawning and see that Dad has parked the tractor. We're home.

"You were sleeping so soundly, Chey. Sorry to have to wake you," Dad says with a smile. "And here are your boys." He nods out toward the fence.

I look out toward the gate. BigHorn and Rocky are standing nose to tail, nibbling each other's backs.

"Yup, told you Rocky would beat us home," I say. "I imagine he's worn out BigHorn's ear telling him about his time at the reservoir."

"I'd think BigHorn has worn out Rocky's, telling him about his amazing race home with you." Dad squeezes my knee. "Now, you bring your boys to the barn, then come on in for some breakfast."

A sudden sadness overtakes me. I turn to climb from the tractor and remind Dad, "I don't know how much boasting a horse like BigHorn can do. No matter how flawlessly he runs, you'll never let me compete on him." I unlatch the door and can feel Dad's eyes on me as I climb down. When I touch the ground and walk to my boys, I say to myself, "In fact, Rocky probably spends all day comforting BigHorn and telling him it doesn't matter what people think."

The two horses raise their heads when they see me and Rocky nickers while BigHorn prances in circles around me. "Come on boys, let's give you two some tasty snacks." After unlatching the wire gate to let Dad through with the tractor, I walk toward the barn. Rocky and BigHorn follow me, no more than a step behind.

I know they're both eager for their grain because each is determined to stay in the lead. They trail behind me like well-behaved children and mimic my movements. I stop suddenly in the road to test them, and they stop immediately in response. I walk again and hear the sound of their hooves pursue me, then I stop once more. Their hooves fall silent. I smile mischievously and begin to start and stop every few steps, and their copycat behavior continues, making me grin from ear to ear. I keep at it until Rocky gives a disapproving snort, as if to say, "Quit it already!" and BigHorn stomps his hooves against the ground with impatience.

"Awwh, did I annoy you boys?" I say teasingly. Chuckling, I turn to give them each a pat.

"Don't worry, you'll both be getting your fair share of oats." As I stand there, though, it occurs to me that my two incredible horses are not in competition for the oats. They are competing for my affection. "Oh my! Aren't you two adorable?" I give them each a good hug before we continue on to the barn.

Mom and Cora wait for us with full buckets. Rocky sees them first and, with a nicker, he ditches me and races to my little sister's treat.

We halter the horses and while they munch on their oats, I hose the mud from Rocky's legs and chest. BigHorn paws the ground with his hooves, demanding the same despite being perfectly clean. "You little jealous bugger," I say.

We turn them out for fresh hay and walk toward the house, Mom and I, each holding one of Cora's hands as we swing her between us.

"Did you see our run back there?" I ask Mom cheerily.

"I caught a glimpse from the window, but you'll have to tell us the entire story in detail at breakfast!" Mom replies, her face glowing with pride. "All I know is that you're one remarkable young lady."

Mom's words make me smile as Cora giggles, flying for a couple of seconds at a time between us, like an astronaut jumping on Mars.

A fire is roaring when we come into the house. Mom has prepared a breakfast feast. I see her famous sausage and egg casserole, and my mouth waters at the smell of her sweet rolls.

Jackson, Francis, and Dad burst into the kitchen talking loudly. "Yeah, if that had happened to me at her age, I surely would have killed the bull, the horse, or myself in that rescue," I hear Dad say. "She's smarter and more crafty than I ever was. " He gives me a wink.

We all sit down together. "Mom, this food looks incredible. Thanks for making all of this. I'm starved."

Mom smiles and replies, "You deserve it. You're a hero today."

Mom places two sweet rolls on my plate while Jackson says, "Tell us the story, Chey. We're all so excited to hear about your holesome rescue. Get it? Hole-some? Like wholesome without a 'w'?"

Mom shakes her head, depositing two sweet rolls onto Jackson's plate to distract him from cracking more terrible puns.

Dad sets his fork down and scoots his chair back. He turns to me and says, "Before you tell them the story, I've been meaning to tell you something Chey. Before all of this happened today I wanted to tell you that I'm sorry."

Confused, I freeze midbite, sweet roll in the air. I set my roll down and look at Dad.

Dad scoots in close and picks up both of my hands. "Your mom and I spoke last night and she helped me to understand that you ***are*** strong enough to defend BigHorn. I wanted to tell you that you do have what it takes to run BigHorn in the rodeo. Your performance this morning further proved that point."

"But Dad, I thought you said the crowds wouldn't cheer for me on him..."

Dad doesn't let me complete my sentence before he says, "I saw you riding down the fence line. I have never in my life witnessed a run like that. I counted the times you and BigHorn touched the ground on one hand. You have a true athlete, an athlete with an incredible ability to run. It takes extraordinary love to accept a horse like BigHorn, and it takes an exceptional rider to ride such a horse. A rider as good as you," he says. Squeezing my hand, he goes on. "You two looked so perfect racing, no one would dare to

make fun of you, nor your horse. And if they do, you are strong enough to tell them to keep their jealous comments to themselves. You can stick up for yourself and for BigHorn, and I'll be there to back you up should you need me."

Happiness swells up inside of me like a balloon; I can't believe the words coming out of Dad's mouth. I return Dad's squeeze and say, "BigHorn and I are ready to run. With you behind us, Dad, we can't be beat."

Looking to Jackson, I reassure him, "You keep roping on BigHorn. He's a strong enough horse for both of us."

Jackson smiles through a mouthful of sweet rolls, crumbs sprinkling down his chin. A moment of blissful silence settles over the room as everyone begins to reach for their food.

Piping up suddenly, Francis says, "How goes that story you's gonna tell us, Chey?"

I smile and lean forward to begin my tale.

INTERVIEW WITH THE AUTHOR

1) What inspired you to write your book?
I was inspired by my kids and how they interacted with their new horse BigHornCatchMeQuick.

2) When did you decide to become a writer?
I began to write stories in the 4th grade and have written ever since.

3) What are some of the major themes of this book? Why did you pick these themes?
Being different is not strange; being different is unique. I picked this theme because we all, horses included, tend to treat others who are different poorly. The second theme of the story is that it is okay to stand up for yourself and those you care about when they are being treated bad. I chose this theme because oftentimes I see young people being bullied and teased, and kids don't feel that they can defend themselves.

3) Is there a BigHorn in real life?
Yes

4) Who is Cheyanna?
Cheyanna is based on the blending of three people that I love: my two girls and their grandmother when she was young.

5) Which character do you relate to most?
I relate most to Bea, the mom. Not just because I'm also a mother, but because I prefer rock'n'roll over country music.

6) Do you think horses feel the same way humans do?
Absolutely! Horses remind me of little kids who haven't exactly learned how to share their feelings.

7) Do non-disabled horses notice a difference with a disabled horse and would they treat it differently?
Yes! Horses are terrible about isolating the weaker animal off from the herd. Every once in a while, you'll come across a horse that doesn't care about the difference in another horse. BigHorn and Rocky, for example, grew to be the best of friends because they were both outcasts. BigHorn, because of his disfigurement (he could not breathe from his nose this is how horses greet one another) and Rocky because he was old.

8) Why a horse with disabilities and not a person?
Watching my other horses when I brought BigHorn home pick on him and push him away was like watching society under a microscope. I was inspired by them and knew that horses could be likable as characters.

9) What are some myths about horses with tracheotomies?

I have been asked repeatedly if BigHorn is susceptible to pneumonia. This must be a myth, because that has never been an issue with BigHorn.

10) What writers inspire you?

CS Lewis, known for *The Lion, the Witch, and the Wardrobe* and JRR Tolkien who wrote *The Hobbit*, *The Lord of the Rings*, and many others are my two greatest inspirations.

11) What draws you to this genre?

I love and live the western genre, and mostly am drawn to writing stories for and about young girls.

12) Why do you write?

Creative expression is a human need that we all must fill, and I have been blessed with words as my medium.

13) What is your advice for dealing with someone like Dad in the story, who can't look past a person's disability?

The dad in the story was afraid. He was afraid of what others would say and how they would treat Cheyanna. His fears were based on his experiences as a kid. Communication is always the first tool in dealing with someone and their prejudices. Find out why they feel the way they do and then try to educate them. Knowledge is the door to kindness. People can be mean simply because they don't know or understand, and fear is a safety mechanism when faced with the unknown.

14) What advice do you have for a kid who might be struggling with insecurity or disabilities?

You are not alone! Everyone has struggles and insecurities. There is always someone who is having a much harder time than you, so look around and count your blessings.

Reader Chat

Discussion Guide

1) If you were Cheyanna, how would you react to BigHorn?

2) What are the themes in this story?

3) What is the moral of this story?

4) Who was your favorite character and why?

5) Who was your least favorite character and why?

6) Do you know any animals with disabilities?

7) Why do you think it was so easy for Jackson to accept BigHorn but hard for Cheyanna?

8) What specific passages struck you as significant, interesting, profound, amusing, disturbing, memorable and/or sad? And why?

9) What have you learned after reading this book?

10) Why do you think the author wrote this book?

11) Do the characters seem real and believable? Can you relate to their predicaments? To what extent do they remind you of yourself or someone you know?

12) Did certain parts of the book make you uncomfortable? If so, why did you feel that way?

13) What was your favorite part of the story?

14) If you could have any of the animals as a pet, who would be and why?

15) Did you like the book? Why or why not?

16) What did you think of the ending? Did you think it made sense to end the novel this way? Why or why not?

17) Why do you think Cheyanna made the choice she did?

18) What did you think of the plot line development?

19) Have your parents ever shared a childhood story with you to help you make a decision, like Mom did with Cheyanna?

20) Did you think Cheyanna's father could have been a little more sympathetic and understanding toward BigHorn's condition?

21) How do you think Francis's disability affects his relationship with the animals?

22) Do you sympathize with any of the characters? Whom and why?

23) Do you think Cheyanna's decision to give Rocky to Cora was a good decision? Why or why not?

24) What do you think about the book cover? Was it appealing?

25) Would you recommend this book to your peers?

CPSIA information can be obtained at www.ICGtesting.com
Printed in the USA
LVOW04s2333300815

452125LV00015B/123/P